Emotive

Emotive

Kevin Laymon

Printed in the United States of America

First Printing, 2016

Edited by Danielle Fisher

Published by Ikigai Publishing ™

www.AuthorKevinLaymon.com

www.Twitter.com/Kevin_Laymon

www.Facebook.com/AuthorKevinLaymon

www.Instagram.com/Kevin_Laymon

Table of Contents

Emotive is dedicated to all of the friends
I have known that time has since forgotten.

He backed away from me and left me with my now dead friend. As much as I wanted retribution, there was no fight left in me. I was defeated.

Dear reader,
keep pressing forward.

ACT I

DABDA

(The Kübler-Ross Model)

Chapter 1

Swing Life Away

The pendulum swayed at a rhythm that echoed eternity in my mind. That great grandfather clock, oh how I hated it, yet no other inanimate object lay within this house that I depended on more...Well, aside from my water dish.

Yeah, I guess I am a little thirsty. Maybe I will go have a drink. Meh, why bother?

The hardwood floor was cold, but I had been laying on my belly for so long that the spot directly below had become cozy and warm.

The wind howled and carried on all afternoon. It sang a song that my ancestors once cried out to the moon many generations ago. The season was winter and that meant that the outside air stung my face. Snow would also get caught in my black and brown mane, but I did not care. While my list of favorite things was long and diverse, playing in the snow was one of my all-time favorite things to do.

I sat inside all day, for I was alone and waiting.

The grandfather clock in the corner of the room sounded off with three chimes that reverberated across the walls with a deep and distant tone. It was not that long ago that the large clock sounding off every hour would frighten me. Ignorance really. Sometimes when we do not understand what something is or how it works, we become afraid of it. It seems silly to be afraid of a clock when I look back and reflect on it. Though, in my defense, I stood by the notion that those bells were sinister in nature.

While I kept my face flat on the floor, I raised my eyes up to my brows to stare at it.

Hmmm. It needs to go off two more times before Sam comes home. That's okay. I am sure he is busy, probably buying a new tennis ball for us to play with or something.

In time, I gave into my dreariness and succumbed to a deep slumber for the remainder of the afternoon. I dreamed of a farm. I could not know for sure, but something told me that this place that I saw so vividly in my mind was once my home. Perhaps when I was too young to form long standing memories, something got caught within the web that is my brain and was lying dormant until the time allowed for such remembrance.

Although a wooden fence staked into the ground established a parameter for just how far they could go, horses ran across fields of green and yellow. Fall was in the air. The scent of apples ripening and leaves changing confirmed this suspicion to be true. I looked off past the fields with the horses to see hills pixelated in orange, gold, and brown. The trees of the foreign landscape were enduring the changing of seasons and, in turn, changing their colors.

Behind me was a very large and very red house. As much as I wanted to enter and investigate it, I could not. Some unknown force was stopping me from journeying in toward the direction which my curiosity desired to lead.

I looked down at my legs, which felt like jelly. They shook when I tried to move them. It was then that I noticed my body was far smaller than I was used to. Perhaps this dream was of a time just after birth.

I could smell other dogs of the same pack. They were family. Though I could not see their faces, I knew they were there. The overwhelming scent wafted through the air of someone I knew quite well and yet could not see. It was my mother. No matter how hard I tried to see her, I could not make out her blurry silhouette. I wanted so badly to see her face, to touch her nose with mine, but it was clear that in this dream, I was not in control.

I began to whine and whimper as things quickly began to feel uncomfortable. The shadow of my mother and her pups was disappearing with the brightness of the setting sun over the hillside. The light felt as though it were burning away at my body and soul as I yelped out louder than before for help. No one seemed to hear my cries or, if they had heard, they simply didn't care of my agony.

Suddenly, overcome with the intense rush of falling, I awoke to the sound of a truck pulling into the driveway. I spared no time leaping up off the floor and was at the door faster than a hummingbird swooping in for nectar in the springtime. My emotions of fear quickly surged into that of excitement as I jumped up and down to try and peer out of the big window in the kitchen.

I could see Sam and he was just sitting in his truck!

What is he doing? Doesn't he know that I am in here waiting for him?

I began to whine with excitement. How immature of me -I know- to whine like a little puppy. I mean, I was eight whole months old after all, an adult, and it was time for me to start acting like it!

It's okay, he is coming. I reassured myself as I began to pace back and forth.

After about five minutes, the door to Sam's truck slammed shut and I jumped up again to look out of the big window in the kitchen. This time I could see him making his way through the snow towards the house.

Suddenly I froze at the sound of liquid hitting the floor. This was my doing. I couldn't help it. I had just pissed all over the floor. It was then that my excitement to see Sam quickly turned to disappointment. Not in him, of course, but myself, for I knew I had let him down.

The front door pricked open, bringing with it the wind and cold from the outdoor wintery weather. Still partially excited to see Sam, I wagged my tail, all the while hanging my head in shame for what I had done.

"Linus! What the fuck?" Sam let out with anger.

Before I could react, he smacked me in the mouth. I did not see it coming and let out a yelp in both surprise and pain. As I took off for another room, he grabbed me by the collar and dragged me back to my mess. I cried as he slammed my snout into the puddle of urine and rubbed my face in it.

"Bad dog, Linus!" Sam exclaimed with a ferocious sense of masculinity in his voice. He opened the door and didn't have to do much to get me outside. The way I saw it, getting my face out of my own urine and into the stinging cold snow was a best case scenario kind of thing.

***

The next day I met Sam downstairs in the kitchen for breakfast. It was his day off and we were to go to the park and play in the snow. After he devoured his steak and eggs, he ushered me out the door.

It's okay. I wasn't very hungry anyway. I am just excited for a day of play!

I raced him to his truck. Victorious as always, I paced back and forth waiting for him to open the door and help me up inside.

He clicked in the door's frozen handle and pried it open, then stood staring at me. "Let's go," he commanded.

Usually he picks me up and helps me in, but not today, I guess. I was too big for that now. I scrunched my butt up and lowered my chest to the ground so that I could spring up and in, but in executing my plan I fell short. Only my front legs and chest made it into the truck.

"You fatass," Sam chuckled.

After leaving me vulnerable in a moment of embarrassment, he lifted me up and into the truck and we were on our way.

Sitting upright in the passenger seat of the old, white Nissan, I could just see out of the windows.

Perfect, I thought with excitement.

This winter had been brutally cold but, on that particular day, all was right and well with the world. The sun was out and the front yard was glistening.

We pulled out of the driveway and onto the slushy, wet road. We then began our ride down the block. As we passed by all the different houses, my imagination was overwhelmed with what may lay inside each and every building of various shape and size.

There was one house in particular I would always remember. Exactly six houses down the street from ours was a great victorian castle of a home. A massive door served as the great entrance to whatever king and queen must have resided within. What caught my attention to the house the first time I saw it but a few weeks ago wasn't the beauty of the structure, but rather the beauty of one of its residents. It was a female who was the same species as I. With a beautiful brown and black mane that was superior to my own, she was much older than I. Perhaps she herself was the queen to that incredible domain.

We passed the mansion and I cocked my head around, looking for her. I had only really seen her once, but that single moment was enough to force me to check for her each time thereafter.

We continued down the street for a couple of blocks and then made a right. The park was not much further off. With every passing house, I tried to calculate just exactly where we were, but somewhere I lost my bearings. Before I knew it, we were pulling up to the park and I completely lost my train of thought as I sat upright and began wagging my tail.

Sam put his chin on the steering wheel and scoped out the scene for a minute. There were plenty of children out and about today. Some were making a snowman, others riding sleds, and a few even rolling around on the ground. I couldn't wait to get out there. Maybe Sam would let me play with the kids today. He usually would.

Sam got out of the driver's side door and pulled a pack of cigarettes out from one of his black jacket's many pockets. He tossed one of the sticks into his mouth and lit it up.

He could have let me out while he did that, but that's okay, I can wait.

A tall, thin, blonde-haired girl bundled up in a silly-looking puffy jacket was coming down a clear cement path from just over a large hill that fed into the park. She was carrying a handful of books. If I remember correctly, Shawna was her name and she was twenty-three years old. She attended the local state college. Sam and I visited this park often and this was not the first time we had seen this girl.

He opened the door to the truck while taking one final puff of his cigarette. After flicking the stick off into the wind, he exhaled a cloud of smoke into my direction.

Nauseating. I wish you wouldn't do that. You know I hate the smell of that stuff.

Sam reached into one of the side compartments on the inside of the truck's door and withdrew a pack of gum. Tossing a piece quickly into his mouth, he looked at himself in the rearview mirror. He slicked back his black hair and ran his fingers over his smooth, clean-shaven face. He then dove further into the truck so that he could reach into the glove box. He withdrew a can of spray that smelled far more wretched than the stench of smoke that clung to his clothing.

I think women are supposed to be attracted to the disgusting scent of the spray or something.

"Showtime," Sam said with a twisted sort of smile.

I hesitated for a second to jump down from the truck. It looked so high up- like looking down from the peak of a mountain in some distant land-suddenly my train of thought was besieged as I was overwhelmed with vertigo. Sam had nudged me on down and I was not anticipating as such. I bit my tongue as I landed on my chest, but that's okay. I was now out of the truck and on the ground, ready to play.

I wonder if he brought the ball. I hope he did.

I looked up to him and he pulled out a yellow tennis ball that he had stuffed in his jacket. He must have read my mind. I became overwhelmed with excitement. That yellow tennis ball is, after all, one of my most favorite of things.

He launched it through the air in the direction of the girl, Shawna, who was approaching, and I was off like a leopard running through the snow drifts. It was difficult, but I did not let up as I trotted forward. All would be worth it when I could triumphantly harbor that yellow tennis ball once more in my mouth for all to witness.

I reached the general area where it had landed. I wished I was fast enough to have made it in time to catch the ball before it disappeared into the snow, but that was okay. I just had to sniff it out. I knew its smell; rubbery like the soles of Sam's shoes, yet fibery like the small rug by the back door. I picked up the scent of Sam and his cigarette that clung to the ball and locked onto its general direction. I buried my face in the snow to chomp around until I blindly grasped onto the toy. I then pulled my face back up to the surface where I was met by

Shawna.

"Look at you," she said with a giggle. "Your face is completely covered in snow."

Yeah, well, I had to get my ball.

She brushed my nose clear of a bit of the powder while continuing to laugh. "May I?" she asked as she held out her hand for my ball.

Sorry, I have got to get this back to Sam.

I turned around and began trotting on back when I noticed Sam was coming our way. He was only a few feet away.

"Give her the ball, Linus," he commanded.

Okay...Well, if that is what you want.

I turned and looked back up at her as she continued to smile down at me. Her face, though mostly wrapped up in a scarf, radiated with joy.

Okay. Yeah, sure. Here ya go.

I placed the ball in the palm of one of her gloved hands and she rubbed the top of my head with a smile.

"You are just so adorable."

Sure...Whatever...Just throw the ball, please.

She tossed it as far as she could. Not quite as far as Sam could throw it, but I was off in pursuit nonetheless. This time I saw where it had landed. It was once again buried deep within the soft afternoon snow. I did not hesitate to dive right in after it. After a few seconds of chomping around, I withdrew my face triumphantly from the mound of powder and began my jog back to the two who were now conversing.

"Well, yeah, we were just getting out of here, let me give you a ride," Sam offered.

Wait what? But we just got here, Sam.

"I don't know...I mean I don't mind walking. I do it every day," she said, sounding uncomfortable with the kind offer.

"No, come on. It's cold out," he added persistently with a fake smile.

Shawna looked to the ground and clenched her books

tightly up against her chest. She glanced over to me. I was still holding the tennis ball waiting for one of them to take it and continue playing.

"Yeah. Okay," she agreed.

"Come on, Linus," Sam called as he walked back to the truck with Shawna.

He opened the door and lifted me up and into the truck and I took a seat, disappointed in the shortness of our adventure.

"Give her room, Linus," Sam said as he pulled me into the center so that Shawna could take my window seat.

The two of them were silent as Sam started up the truck and pulled out onto the road. We drove up the street for a minute or two and I could sense the awkwardness that floated about the cabin of the vehicle. It lingered for the duration of the trip home.

"I am just up here by the light," Shawna said, breaking the silence and pointing ahead to an intersection.

I flopped down and hung my head over the edge of the seat with a sigh.

I can't believe we were only at the park for two, literally two, ball throws.

"Oh, it's right here," Shawna said. "You passed it."

Keeping my head hung low, I scanned the floor of the truck and watched the bits of snow slowly dissolve in the blast of hot air from the heater. It was odd to watch them die off as if they had never even existed.

"What are you doing? Please stop the car," she added in a tone of urgency. She was beginning to panic and sounded alarmed.

What do you mean what am I doing? I am just looking at the floor.

"Just relax, okay?" Sam said, entering the conversation. "Play it cool and I will not hurt you."

Oh...She was talking to him, not me. Okay, never mind

then.

"No, no, no. Please, please, please stop the car," Shawna pleaded as her sense of worry elevated.

It's a truck, lady.

I heard the high-pitched sound of a blade drift through the air behind my head. I turned to see that Sam had reached over and stuck the knife that he kept in his jacket up against the girl's side.

"Keep calm, and everything will be just fine," he reassured her with emphasis on his authoritative tone.

Seeing the blade pressed up tightly against her coat, Shawna began to cry and sniffle as we pulled into our driveway.

Sam looked through the back window and then pulled out a roll of duct tape from underneath his seat. He sat the roll of tape up on the dash, directly in front of Shawna, then instructed her to give him her hands.

"Please no," she sniffled. "I have to get home. My friends are waiting for me," she explained as she succumbed to a full-blown cry. Gasping for air in between chokes of tears and snot, she was quick to lose her sense of cool.

"Give me your fucking hands," Sam repeated in an angry tone as he dug the blade deeper into her side.

The tip of the knife punctured the girls puffy jacket and she responded to his request by raising her arms into the air. Sam wrapped her hands tightly together with the tape, then placing a final strip around her face, Sam sealed off her mouth to prevent the girl from speaking.

"Alright, we are going to get out of the truck now and walk to the house. If you try to run away, I will bleed you dry in the driveway. Understand?"

She had her eyes closed and cried like a child. I am not even sure she was capable of answering, but after he repeated himself in anger, she gave a muffled nod of acceptance.

Sam jumped out of the truck and walked around to the passenger door. She gave me a look as if pleading with me, but

I really wasn't sure what she could want from me in the odd little game that they were playing.

"Let's go," Sam growled as he opened the passenger side door.

He then pulled the girl out of the truck. The books she had on her lap fell to the ground and into the snow. He paid no mind to the fallen books as he escorted her up to the house and left me to myself in the truck.

Okay, you got this, I thought, as I focused on the snow covered books as a target. I scrunched my butt up in the air, preparing to jump from the truck on my own.

Three...Two...One...Liftoff.

I hit the ground but forgot to bend my knees, which was a bit painful, but luckily I hit the books as planned. They crunched deeper into a snow pile that was still soft and fresh, absorbing most of the blow. I ran up to the house and stopped at the door, but I could not see the two of them through the window.

Great, who knows how long I will be stuck out here alone now.

I turned around and looked out into the snow-covered yard, where flakes gently fell from the sky and began compiling quickly on the steps below me.

I wonder how many snowflakes are out here. Probably hundreds of billions, maybe more. How many is a billion, even?

Suddenly, a small brown lump of rapid, sporadic movement caught my attention.

Hey, who are you? I barked to a small, fluffy-tailed rodent who scurried across the driveway with an acorn stuffed in his mouth.

That acorn is from our yard, you cannot have that, I continued to bark. *Put that back under the snow where you found it!*

Midway through my rant, the door to the porch flung open and Sam stepped outside.

Uh oh, now you have done it, little rodent, Sam is going

to be pissed you have been stealing his acorns, he is going to-

"Linus!" Sam yelled, "Get your ass inside!"

Oh right, okay. Sorry.

I scurried into the house and over to the living room. Sam followed me in and turned on the television for Shawna. She was sitting in a chair looking sweaty and anxious with the tape still over her hands and mouth. I ran over to the couch and climbed up to join the two of them in watching TV.

What are we watching? Ooh, Groundhog Day? Oh, I love this movie! I especially like the part towards the end where Bill Murray takes the groundhog for a ride in his car. Wait a second, is today Groundhog Day? I'm not so good with dates, but if it is Groundhog Day shouldn't we go out, check see if the little rodent eyes his shadow?

I looked over to the two of them. Sam was kneeling in front of Shawna. He rammed his knife into the coffee table and began to speak quietly. "Listen to me, okay?"

She nodded her head with tears swelling from her frightened, wide eyes.

"I'm not going to hurt you, okay? I'll take this tape off your mouth if you promise not to scream."

Scream? Why would she scream? She seems like such a sweet and gentle girl.

Again she nodded.

The sound of the tape ripping away from her face raised the hairs on the back of my neck.

You should consider yourself lucky to not have fur like me, or else you would have lost a handful to that wretched stuff. I despise tape. A few months ago, I got some of that junk stuck on the bottom of my paw. It was perhaps the most painful experience in my entire life when Sam tore it away.

She continued to sob while directing an empty stare towards the floor. Sam gently placed a hand on to her leg, which captured the attention of her innocent gaze. He began to stroke at the inner thigh of her pants.

"You have the most perfect set of hips. Has anyone ever told you that? It is what caught my eye the very first time we met." He paused to stretch the tips of his fingers around the upper portion of her leg as if surveying it. "It was difficult to tell, with you bundled up for your walks in the cold, but now I can see that my initial assumptions of your curvature hold true. It's an exciting thing, really." Again he paused as his hands made their way down to the lower portion of her leg. "Below the knee caps though, not so good. A little too thick, so we will have to do without that part of the meal."

The comment seemed to confuse her and again her light cry broke into a heavier one.

"Shawna," he said dragging out the sound of the letters that spelled her name, "What did I say about being *quiet*?"

"Please," she begged, "Let me go and I won't tell anyone. Please!"

"Or you could stay and not tell anyone," he added with a smirk. "It has been so long since I have had the company of a woman. I guess my abilities in seduction are rusty," he finished as he continued caressing her thigh.

He picked up the blade buried into the coffee table and ran it up against the tape that bound her hands together. He looked directly into her eyes, then, slicing the strips loose, he freed her hands. He tossed the steel back onto the table, then he took her hands in his and ran them up to his face.

"So soft is the skin of a beautiful young woman," he pointed out as he closed his eyes and sighed.

Her eyes drifted over to the blade that rested three to four feet away.

"Why don't you take that off," he suggested of her coat. "Get comfy and relax."

Slowly, she removed her jacket, then she abruptly threw it at his face and lunged forward for the blade on the table. As if anticipating her move, he discarded the jacket and stood with her. He swung her around like a helpless little ragdoll and, holding her tight within his arms, he dipped down to the floor with her. In the struggle, she smashed the side of her head against the table and gave into his power as she drifted motionlessly to the ground.

Feeling uneasy with the situation, I jumped off the couch and joined them on the floor.

Shawna's face was parallel to the floor and her soggy eyes, sad and desperate, looked into mine.

Sam... I'm not so sure that she is so enthused with what you are doing.

The room felt as though it were darkening. The sun was setting outside, but the lack of light was not the cause of unease that set over us in that moment.

Blood trickled down the side of Shawna's head; it rolled up over her eye and through her brow before dripping down onto the floor.

I think she is hurt, Sam, stop it! I barked, as he began rubbing her shoulders.

"I just want to get to know you, Shawna. I like you. Don't you like me, too?"

Sam, stop it! She is hurt, I continued to bark as I watched her continue to bleed from the head.

"Linus," Sam roared, looking up to me with fire in his eyes.

It wasn't like me to rebel against his authority, he was after all the alpha male in our domain, but something was wrong, Shawna was hurt, and it seemed as though he could not see that.

Sam picked the blade up off the table and jammed it into his belt, then he snatched me up by the collar. Caught off guard, I yelped and squirmed as he dragged me with ease off into the back room and slid me across the floor. Trying to grip the hardwood floor with my paws, I slipped like a spoon to wet noodles. The door slammed shut just as I reached it and I clawed helplessly at the knob.

No! Wait! Don't leave me in here!

The room was dark and the only source of light was that which peaked in from under the door from out in the living room. It cast eerie shadows in all directions that flickered to life and terrified me to the core. Images of spiders erupting by the thousands from the wound of a stagnant corpse were accompanied by maggots that squirmed about as they feasted on the flesh of the obscure dead. I sank to the floor in defeat. I didn't want to look at the creepy shadows, but also could not get my eyes low enough to see through the crack under the door. I could hear clearly the conflict unfolding in the living room and figured it best to focus on that as to not feed my imagination with the shadows that lingered all around me.

"Where you going, Cutie?" Sam cynically cackled.

I heard a loud thud in the kitchen, which suggested someone attempting to make it out of the door of the house had fallen hard to the ground. The crash was immediately followed by the high pitch screams of Shawna.

"Somebody! Please help me!"

Her cries gave me goosebumps that made me feel anxious and helpless as I sat locked behind the door, left only to my own assumptions of sensibility.

More crashing suggested the strife was leading up towards the door of the house, which lie just outside the kitchen.

Shawna could be heard crying as she softly mumbled the words "please" over and over and over again.

One final scream to embody every single drop of the girl's frustration and terror bellowed through the house with a hair-raising screech that forced me to flinch and jump back, away from the door. I moved over to the darkest corner of the room and huddled to myself. I had heard enough and was no longer curious as to the affairs of the two outside.

I tried to go to sleep. Even though all was now eerily quiet within the house, my conscience simply would not allow me to drift off and away from reality. I was stuck to my own sense of self; trapped within my own mind. I clenched my eyes tightly shut as to not see the chaotic shadows that engulfed my prison and amplified my fear.

Chapter 2

Creep

As the sun came up, it gifted me with the shine of its light into the room that I was trapped within all evening. In being granted the light, I realized I actually was not trapped at all. There was a second door on the far side of the room that led into a bathroom and that bathroom fed into the kitchen. Feeling foolish, I slowly got up from my night of fear and sulking to make my way out into the kitchen.

Sam had spent the entire night stowed away in the basement. I am not sure what exactly it was he was doing down there, but it must have been important. Throughout the course of the night, I occasionally woke to the sounds of his power tools roaring to life from time to time. I could only assume he was building something.

Always constructing things, that Sam. A damn shame his

day job wasn't something more creative. I'm not sure what exactly his career field was; something physical in a warehouse with a boss he despised and coworkers that teased him. That was the extent to which I knew about his job. Regardless, so much wasted potential.

I made way into the living room and climbed up onto the couch. Though her scent strongly lingered as if she were standing before me, the truth was Shawna was nowhere in sight. I suppose I must have slept through the sound of her leaving the house.

It was well past the time for breakfast, but still Sam was drilling and sawing away in the basement. I tried to take my mind off of food and walked over to the window where I saw the squirrel from yesterday inside Sam's truck. Sam had left the passenger side door open and the persistent rodent had taken advantage of the opportunity to go inside.

Hey you! Get out of there, I barked, jumping at the window.

My yelling had no effect; the rodent acted as though he couldn't hear me, even though I knew bloody damn well he saw me barking at him. Self-centered pricks, those squirrels, always messing with what is not theirs.

I heard something slam downstairs in the basement and my senses told me Sam was on his way up. I left the window and the squirrel to go over to the basement door so that I may greet Sam as he arrived. The clicks and clanks of a lock in place on his side of the door sounded off as he disengaged the bolts of security. Why he needed all of that seemed silly, he did after all have me, and I'm the greatest guard dog ever.

"What's wrong, Linus?" he asked, peeking his head from around the cracked door.

Nothing's wrong. Why would anything be wrong?

He cautiously opened the door further and with it came a draft from the basement. I was thrown back by the overwhelming scent of blood. No smell is more distinct to a dog than that of blood. I'm told my ancestors once lusted for it. While the smell of it sickened me, my ability to distinguish it from all other smells left me curious.

After squeezing his way out, Sam shut the door behind himself. His eyes were sunken in and darkened. He had been awake throughout the entire night down in that basement. And now that the night had shifted into morning, it was well over twelve hours in total that he had been dispersed alone to his work in that dank, musty, dark cellar.

He went over to the cabinets in the kitchen, took out a glass, and then grabbed some ice from the freezer. The shards of frozen water fell into the glass with a clink, then he took a carton of milk out of the fridge and poured it over the ice. Just as soon as the glass was full, again was it empty as he slammed it down on the table with a sigh of satisfaction.

"I gotta head out for a bit, do you have to go outside?"

Do I ever! I thought you would never ask.

He opened the door and I bolted outside as he lit a cigarette and laced up his boots in preparation for his journey out in the cold.

I sniffed around for a bit before finding the utmost perfect spot to take a leak, *ahh something quite satisfying about taking a pee in the snow*. My right leg grew tired and began to wobble. I was standing in place urinating for longer than usual, but I hadn't gone since early yesterday morning. Having held in my need to pee for so long meant today's trip outside was one of the most relieving experiences in the history of ever.

When I finished, I sniffed around for the scent of the squirrel that tampered with things that were not his, but when I saw Sam open the front door I ran up before he could verbally summon me to avoid angering him.

I knew the routine; it was time for me to go inside and spend the afternoon at home while he was away. *That's okay, maybe he poured me some breakfast.* I flew in through the door. *Shit... He did not leave me any food.* I turned around to see the door slam shut. I walked over to the window whilst letting out a long drawn-out moan. My tummy growled and I was beyond famished.

I watched through the glass as Sam approached his truck. He stopped for a moment, dead in his snowy tracks, as he noticed the passenger door was left open all throughout the day and night prior leading up to this moment.

"Fuck," he yelled loud enough for me to hear through the glass.

He got in the truck and tried to start it a handful of times before pounding on the dashboard like some raging ape and ultimately getting out. He then came back inside holding his cellphone to his face.

"Hey, Mia, yeah listen, are you busy? Cool, well the battery in my truck is dead and I was wondering if you could swing by quick and give me a jump? I don't know... yeah. Okay. Sure, see ya then."

After returning his cellphone back to his pocket, he flopped into a chair at the table and let out a sigh whilst folding his arms.

I could tell that he was angry, but his anger was not directed towards me, but rather at his frustration with the truck. I approached and sat beside him. He reached a hand down to my face and began scratching my head just behind the ears.

Thanks, you know I love that.

After a few minutes, he stopped and I began licking his fingers. They tasted of latex and bleach.

"Knock it off," he wailed as he pulled his hand back to himself.

Right, sorry.

We sat in silence for a few minutes, which was nice, then I walked over to my food dish. I figured now would be as good a time as ever to ask for breakfast, seeing as Sam was just sitting in the kitchen anyway. I shot him a look of pleading and his eyes, dark and angry, drifted across the room to meet mine.

"Hungry?" he questioned with his brows slanted and arms still folded.

Yes, I really, really am.

He stood up and walked over to a small tin trash can where my food was securely stored away from mice and insects that conspire to consume it. He lifted the lid and with it came the contained aroma of turkey and gravy. I began to uncontrollably wag my tail with excitement and anticipation. As soon as the first piece of kibble hit the dish, my face was buried. I was inhaling the meal of ground turkey flavored bites as fast as I could. It annoyed Sam that I could not wait. While allowing my primitive instincts to take over is always an embarrassing show of character, in that moment, I did not care. All was right with the world.

A minute or two passed and, with my dish now empty, I noticed the awkward silence in the room that followed my food-devouring rampage. Sam exhaled a cloud of smoke from where he was sitting at the table behind me. I turned to face him only to see that his tired, sunken eyes were beaming at me while he mouthed at a cigarette. I'm not sure why, but in that moment I felt extremely uncomfortable, as if I had done something terribly wrong, something morbid and on the edge of evil by definition. I drooped my tail between my legs and hung my head low. The room was becoming cold- as if all life within were being drained out by a man in a dark cloak with a scythe. Death, fear, anger, and hatred were together conversing madness between the two of us as oblivion descended an endless sense of chaos upon existence.

I whimpered and, just as soon as I had, a knock on the door reinstated the room of all order and emotion that fit within the norms of reality.

Sam put out his cigarette and jumped up to get the door. It was his sister, Mia. She was bundled up in a puffy brown and pink coat. She wore a matching knitted hat and scarf that disguised her choppy brown hair, but placed emphasis on her beautiful brown eyes. She was a pretty girl. Younger than Sam, in her early twenties, she was already a mother of two, though her figure did little to hint as such.

Still wearing his boots, Sam grabbed his jacket and opened the door.

"Hey," she cheerfully greeted as she backed away from the door.

I was quick to dive through Sam's legs to go outside with them, but he squeezed his knees together, trapping me below.

"Get back inside, Linus," he said with a growl.

Yeah okay, but I can't breathe; you're crushing me.

"Awe, let him come out with us," she suggested, kneeling down to welcome me as Sam released his grip.

I lunged for joy towards her.

"Linus, get down!" Sam yelled.

I backed off, but Mia embraced me anyway as she pulled me closer to pet me and rub her face against mine.

"How you doin', Cutie? I have missed you."

I'm okay, I have missed you too, and the kids, where are they?

I really enjoyed playing with Mia's two children. They were such sweet kids with a limitless reservoir of energy at their exposure. They could play for hours on end.

I licked her face. She couldn't help but giggle and squirm with her eyes tightly shut. Sam brushed past us, hopping off the porch and into the snow with a crunch. He then popped the hood of his truck and withdrew a pair of jumper cables.

"Alright, go run around, you crazy buffoon," Mia said to me with a chuckle as she left to join her brother, who was now attaching the cables to the guts of his truck.

"So, how ya been?" she asked after leaning up against his Nissan.

"Fine," he said coldly as he raised the hood of her car to connect both of the vehicles together.

It was a little too cold to play in the snow, so I took a seat upright to watch the two of them converse. I scanned the ground as the wind howled and fussed about. In its anger, it took with it drifts of powdered snow across the yard.

"Haven't heard from you in a while," Mia stated, trying to guilt Sam into talking to her.

"Yeah well, I have been busy."

"Still, we live right down the street. You could at least pick up your phone from time to time."

"Mia, don't do this right now, please, I have a lot on my mind."

"Yeah okay. Sorry," she said looking down into the snow.

Something beneath her feet had captured her attention and she reached down to uncover the buried treasure that had fallen out of the truck the day before. It was Shawna's two textbooks.

"Are you taking some college courses?" Mia asked just as Sam was about to enter his truck.

"What? No. Why would I be-" he paused as his look of confusion quickly turned into that of concern. Jumping out of the truck, he continued in a vexed tone, "What is that?"

"College course textbooks. On the inside, there is a name written in sharpie, Shawna Williams. Do you have a college girlfriend, Sam?" Mia pressed with a smile.

"Yeah, no, I picked 'em up used from the college library for cheap. Just been reading in my down time. Must have fallen out of my truck last night when I was bringing in some groceries."

"Jeez Sam, a textbook for physics level two and another for calculus level three. This is some intricate stuff," she added while flipping through the pages of one of the books.

"I was just curious about the stuff is all," he said calmly as he reached out his hand for them.

"You always had an interest in science," Mia said with a smile as she forked the books over. "Mom always thought you would be an inventor or some type of high profile engineer."

"Yeah, well, mom thought a lot of things now didn't she," he snickered in disgust.

"When is the last time you spoke to her, Sam?"

"Don't start this shit, Mia."

"You know I stay out of the conflict between you and her, but she is really sick, Sam. Her doctor doesn't think that she'll make it through the year."

Sam placed his head against the open frame of the truck, perhaps in an attempt to hide away his now saddened face. "It's her own fault. If she would have left that monster when we were kids, she would not be laid up in that bed today."

"Maybe, Sam, but that shouldn't strip her away from the only family she has left; her children. Especially in her final days. You were always her favorite. I always figured that while I was doing well in school, using it as my escape and such, she had visions of saving you from him. You were the target of his insanity, more often than me, but Mom loved you and she still does. I think she always wanted to escape. She just never knew how."

"Start up your car," Sam said coldly with an underlying tone of authority as he slumped into his truck to turn the key.

Mia let out a sigh and obliged. The chain reaction was his truck resuscitating back to life with the sound of a low-end rumble. This caused me to flinch. Though I really liked cars, something about the giant hunks of machinery coming to life always made me feel slightly uneasy.

Leaving her engine on, Mia got out of her car. "Let's go get some coffee," she suggested as Sam unhooked the cables that bound the two vehicles and dropped their hoods closed.

"I don't have time. I have to run to the hardware store and pick up some things."

"Not until after you go get some coffee with me. We will just call it payment for me coming over here in the cold on my day off," she said.

Sam took a deep breath and exhaled slowly, "Yeah,

okay. Let me just lock Linus up."

Awe man, but I'm just sitting here.

Mia looked over in my direction and I could see the big, wide-eyed conniving smile she had used on Sam to convince him to take her out for coffee. "Bring him along with us."

Oh, yeah! Bring me with you! I have never had coffee before!

I leaned forward into a standing position and flopped my tongue out of the side of my face with excitement. The shift in positioning released a tremendous amount of body heat that I was storing whilst sitting back. The air was freezing and the wind whipped across my face. Flakes of snow caked the lining of my eyes and I shook my face back and forth to free my coat of the chilly powdered water.

"You coming?" Mia asked.

I opened my eyes to see her smiling face down to my level. She laughed and brushed some of the snow from my eyes, then ushered me towards Sam's truck.

"Let's drop my car off at my place and take your truck. The coffee lounge is only a few blocks up from my place so I will walk home from there or you can drop me off before you go to the store."

Hanging from the door of his truck, Sam made eye contact with me. He didn't look mad per se, but he was certainly annoyed. Perhaps he did not want me to come with him to the coffee shop, and if that were the case, I did not want to go. Upsetting him was the least of my intentions.

After a few seconds, he tilted his head inward towards the cabin of the truck. This was my cue to enter and so, without his physical help, I leapt up into the truck.

"All by yourself this time. Good job," he said, praising me as he got in and closed the door behind himself.

His praise was a comforting and rewarding sort of feeling that I rarely had the opportunity of receiving. That made it all the more worthwhile in the end.

Mia pulled out of the driveway and we followed behind her.

Shawna's books were on the seat beside me and it brought the thought over me as to why Sam would lie about the books being his own. *Why would he deny knowing Shawna? Maybe he doesn't want Mia knowing he has a girlfriend?*

The truck's heaters were on full blast. If the sun would not come out and grace us with its warm, shimmering rays, the gust of mechanically divine warmth that the truck produced was as close of a second as there was.

We pulled up to Mia's place, a large, gothic-styled home that housed herself, her husband, and her two children, Jonathan and Timothy. Smoke ruptured from the home's large chimney high above. The windows were closed with the blinds pulled shut, so I could not see inside and scout for my two friends, Jon and Tim. *I really do love those kids.*

After shutting off her car, Mia approached the passenger door of our truck and opened it to hop in. Though only for a brief moment, I felt all the warm air produced by the truck's heaters scurry out of the open door, while the frigid air from outside made haste in entering the truck's cabin. *Funny how fast you adapt to being in the warmth and how much more dramatic a feeling the cold air is in contrast.*

"Kids home with Vince?" Sam asked.

"Yeah. It's his day off too, so he is home watching basketball while they play their video games," she said before clicking in her seatbelt and sitting upright to look out the front window.

"How is he?"

"Good. He is up for a promotion and working towards that currently. You should come over sometime, have a beer and watch a game with him or something. He asks about you."

"I don't drink, and I hate sports. It's for idiots."

"Yes," she said, cutting him off and rolling her eyes. "I know all about your theories of sports being a means of control over the stupid masses," she added in a mocking tone as if she had heard his Orwellian story too many times before to tolerate listening even once more.

A minute or two of awkward silence passed, every second of which felt tenser than the last. I looked out the front window at the drifts of snow that silently bounced off the windshield as we drove down the street.

"I'm sorry, Sam, but it wouldn't kill you to get out and socialize from time to time."

Sam did nothing to respond. His face reflected emptiness. All he did was stare forward as he manipulated the steering wheel to turn the truck into a parking lot. Perhaps he didn't hear her, though I am sure in all reality he had.

"Grab Linus's leash from the glovebox," Sam instructed of Mia as he shut off the engine and patted my head.

Awe man, I hate the leash. Not like I'm gonna run away or anything.

Mia clipped the cord to my color and we exited the truck out into the world ruled over by dreary winter skies.

Calling the snow that littered the sidewalks of the downtown area 'snow' was an inaccurate way to describe the wet chunks of brown and black slosh. I kind of wanted to go investigate the stuff, splash around and play in it a bit, but that would make Sam upset. Besides, I was bound by that stupid leash anyway.

Though I had no idea where our destination lie, I eagerly pulled the group forward.

"Easy, Linus. You are going to rip my arm off," Mia insisted with a chuckle as I tugged at the leash that bound her to me.

Well, keep up, Slowpokes.

"Linus. Knock it off," Sam warned.

Knock what off?-Oh my god! Guys, look! Another dog!

It was some miniature poodle thing whose fur made it look as though it were possibly related to a sheep. I pulled Mia forward towards the other dog and began leaping to gain every extra inch of a lead I could.

I cocked my head to see that Sam had grabbed the cable from Mia. Wrapping his right arm with some of the slack of the cord to give himself a better grip, he jerked the line in back towards himself. He had done it so hard that not only had I stopped, but I actually flew backwards through the air towards him. Being ripped through the air by a cable attached to your neck- that was a painful mistake I would be sure to never make again.

Laying on my side in the wet, dirty slush, I felt foolish. I stood back up with my eyes locked into a position of looking down. I slowly turned to face Sam, who was still holding onto the leash with a look of disgust. My back was to the poodle. As I faced forward to walk alongside Sam and not ahead, I made sure to not make eye contact with the other dog out of embarrassment.

Mia and Sam did some chatting while I sulked for a few minutes until we reached the cafe. The windows were frosty and yet, through their haze, I could see the faces of many warm bodies as they sipped away on their equally warm drinks from inside the shop.

Sam pulled the door open and I proceeded in alongside Mia. Instantly, half of the room's eyes fell upon me.

"Well aren't you just the cutest thing I have ever seen," proclaimed a woman standing behind the coffee bar. She was pouring a drink for someone. In her temporary mesmerization over me, she had unnoticeably overfilled the drink and spilled some of the brown liquid onto herself. "Ouch," she cried as she pulled backwards from the machine that splurged the boiling hot coffee all over her hands.

Sam's face twisted into a faint sort of smile; one that most people couldn't even detect as even actually being there, but I could see it on his face, plain as day.

"Are you okay?" Mia inquired with concern.

"Oh yes. I am fine," the girl eased with a wince as she reached for a cloth and absorbed the liquid spill. "So, french vanilla roast?"

"You know it," Mia said with a smile.

"And what about you, Hun?" the girl said, looking over to Sam.

"Oh right," Mia interrupted. "Natalie, this is my brother, Sam," she added as she raised her arm to accent her lingo with body language.

"Pleased to meet you, Sam," Natalie admitted with a beam that hinted at her admiration of Sam's physical physique.

Sam simply acknowledged introductions with a smile of his own and then answered her question. "I will take a cup of the Jamaican bold, please."

"Sure," Natalie said, reaching for two cups to pour their drinks into. "So what about you?" she added, glancing down to me.

I have never had coffee. I guess I will have what Sam is having.

"This is Sam's dog, Linus. Isn't he adorable?" Mia said of me.

I am not adorable. I am a ferocious feral spirit of ancient antiquity!

After setting down the two cups of coffee for both Sam and Mia, Natalie came out from around the corner. "He is *so* cute," she re-enforced as she scratched my head with her soft fingers. It felt incredible.

OK sure. I am whatever you want me to be if it means you continue scratching me right there.

"If you want cream, sugar, or honey they are all right behind you," Natalie informed us as she raised her hands away from my head to show Sam.

"No. Just black is fine," Sam said.

"Woah. Live dangerously I see," she chuckled. "Well, I too like to live dangerously."

I licked Natalie's hands to suggest she return to petting me immediately.

"Linus, knock it off," Sam casually instructed of me.

"Awe it's okay. He is just a loving little guy, huh?" Natalie said, defending my intrusion.

A flock of college students carrying books and chatting about their epic night before entered the coffee shop and made way for the counter.

"Stick around, will ya?" Natalie asked of me with a wink as she took position behind the bar to take the kid's orders. In her transition, she briefly shot Sam a glance and a smile.

"Come on, let's grab a seat," Mia said.

Sam and I followed her off to the side where the two of them found seats at a small table. I rested upright against my back legs and allowed my eyes the chance to wander around the shop while the two of them conversed. So much was happening in this foreign land that it served as quite the distraction. The shop was dimly lit with lights turned so low that the gloomy cloud-blocked sun had to squeeze its frail shine in through the large glass windows positioned in the front of the boutique. Near the entrance were a line of wooden stools that looked out into the bustling wintery street. Every seat was taken by people who were both laughing and talking. Maybe they really were enjoying their coffee. Maybe they were just grateful to be out of the cold for a minute, or perhaps they truly enjoyed the company of one another.

I turned back to Mia and Sam. Mia was doing most of the talking and she too smiled frequently to accent her level of happiness, while Sam harbored a blank sort of scowl. He didn't hate his sister, but he also didn't love her. That was something I could never really understand because I had always loved Mia.

A bell attached to the door at the front of the shop gently rattled, which suggested that someone had entered. It was a woman. Her face was completely pale and blue from being outside in the stinging cold. Her expression was that of great sorrow. She wore dirty clothing that looked like rags and, even at my distance away from her, I could smell that she was not clean.

Natalie welcomed the drifter with a sad sort of smile. "Hey, Kathy."

"Why hello, Natalie. How are you this morning?"

"I am good. Cider?"

"Yes, please. I have dollar bills today so we don't need to count the change," the woman said as she reached into one of the pockets of her ripped up jacket.

"That's good, but you keep those today, Kathy." Natalie suggested as she placed the warm drink onto the counter.

The woman, Kathy, looked like she was going to tear up. She was more grateful for that cup of hot cider than most anyone else in the shop was grateful to having had waken up alive and well that morning.

"Bless you, Natalie," the woman said with watery eyes.

"Don't mention it. You try and stay warm out there okay, Kathy?"

The woman took a sip of her drink and smiled before taking her leave.

After my eyes made their rounds about the shop one last time, they drifted back over to Mia and Sam, who were still talking.

"So how exactly do you know Natalie?" Sam questioned.

"Outside of here I don't, but I get coffee here every morning after I drop the kids off at school. She graduated college up at SUNY a few years ago and liked the town so much that she decided to stick around."

"She has a pretty face. Reminds me of someone that I used to know," Sam said as he sneaked a glance over to Natalie.

"She is sweet *and* single. You should ask her out."

Sam shot his eyes back to facing Mia. "Na, I can't."

"Psh, why not? Too busy self-loathing your existence

away? If you don't, I will for you," she informed and followed up with raised eyebrows as she awaited his response.

Sam took a sip of his extra black coffee whilst maintaining a cold sort of eye contact with Mia. He did not verbally respond. Maybe he thought she was bluffing or maybe he just didn't care, but after a moment of silence, Mia smirked, stood up, and walked over to Natalie.

The two spoke softly while Sam and I were left to watch and speculate as to what it could be that they were saying.

With a sigh, Sam reached down and scratched my head. *Ah, thanks man. That feels good.*

After leaving the coffee shop, Sam and I dropped Mia off at her home and then ventured over to the hardware store. The place was a warehouse with ceilings so high that elephants could easily live there in herds of hundreds. Sam placed me in a metal cart on wheels so that I would not wonder off. *It stinks not being able to explore this vast wonderland that smells of freshly cut wood and wet paint, but being in the buggy does let me see everything clearly, just in a more claustrophobic-like way.* The lights in the warehouse were brighter than the outdoor sun, which was something I found unnecessarily strange, but who am I to really dictate what is strange and what is normal, right?

Sam piled bags of powdered stone, buckets of an unknown chemical, and various other tools into the cart. Soon I had no room to move, but that was okay. I was complacent with being able to see everybody pass us by. Most people would smile and wave their hands at me. Though I did not know anyone, I understood the smiles. Smiling is a universal gesture which reflects one's emotional level of excitement and happiness. The waving, however, that was something that always appeared dumb to me. It was a gesture I could never fully comprehend. *Why do they do that?*

"Finding everything alright?" a man asked us as he approached. He was wearing a stupid looking apron that smelled of flowers and dirt.

Don't cooks wear aprons?

Sam didn't hear him. He was stuck in a daze staring at the fine print on the side of a sealed bucket.

"Sir?" the man verbally nudged, trying to get Sam's attention.

Still, Sam didn't notice.

Hello, I am Linus.

I wagged my tail and reached out of the cart to lick the man who smelled of flowers and nectar.

"Hey, knock it off," Sam warned.

My fiddling around forced Sam to notice the man I was reaching for.

"Need any help today?" the man asked as he scratched my ears.

Yes. Please get me out of this stupid thing!

"No. We are fine, thank you," Sam informed.

The man smiled, gave me one final scratch, and then walked away.

Damnit. I am still trapped.

Sam decided on the bucket he was holding and stuffed it under the cart.

"Ready to get out of here?" he asked me.

Sure. I have to go pee anyway.

We cashed out and loaded up the truck with all of the newly purchased goods, then set off for home. I didn't know what we would be building, but based on how much stuff Sam had got, I could only imagine it was going to be something magnificent.

While Sam unloaded the truck and brought the things inside, I splashed around in the snow. As the day grew older, the sun's setting rays had spent the afternoon melting some of the fine powder into liquid and it was fun to play with. Trudging through the yard of wet snow felt heavy on my coat, and I imagined that I was a lion being pinned down by an attacking outsider pride. I barked and jumped against the weight of the snow for some time until Sam was all done carrying the things we had purchased inside.

"Come on, Linus," Sam suggested, and I was happy to oblige.

Once inside, I ran towards the fireplace, which was lit and radiating heat. I shook my coat off next to the flame. I used to be afraid of the blaze, but I am older now and far more mature.

Sam entered the room carrying Shawna's books, which he had claimed earlier as his own. He didn't hesitate to toss them into the fireplace and kneel down to watch them as they were consumed by flames.

A sweet fragrance caught my attention. It was one that was not native to our living room, so it proved easy to track down. The source was Shawna's pink, puffy jacket. It was draped across the backside of the far end of the couch. I climbed over to the cushions and buried my face into the coat. It smelled like her, which was a comforting sort of scent.

After watching the books burn to ash, Sam stood up and faced me. Me playing with Shawna's jacket captured his gaze and he was quick to apprehend the coat.

"Watch out," Sam warned.

I jumped off the couch and he snatched up the jacket and rolled it up tightly into a ball before tossing it into the fire.

The books had burned in a similar way to the wood Sam fed the fire on a regular basis: slow and steady with crackling embers. But the jacket caused the inferno to squelch and scream as it roared to life with an array of skewed colors that suggested it was furious with the sacrifice it had been offered. Watching the piece of clothing dissolve into the flames was eerie and uncomfortable, but the ordeal only lasted a minute or two. Then, with a long sigh, Sam hung his head low and disappeared off to the basement.

Left to myself, I whined a little bit. My teeth ached and I felt the urgency to chew on something to satisfy my compulsion. Wandering into the kitchen, I spotted a pair of Sam's shoes.

They were a brown leather dress pair that he would wear out sometimes. *Sam would be irate if I destroyed these, but he has no use for them at the moment. Maybe I will just gnaw on the ends a little.* I chewed on the tough leather, which smelled as marvelous as it felt in my mouth. The gums of my teeth ached in a blissfully addictive sort of way that allowed time to fly by at a ridiculous rate. What felt like seconds were actually hours. Just as soon as I had begun nibbling on one shoe, I found myself ringed with the bits and pieces of both shoes. I had been mesmerized in a moment of euphoric frenzy that had blinded me as I ravaging both of the loafers into fine strips of shredded leather.

In that moment, I froze. I had no idea how I did not hear or sense him prior to then, but Sam had surfaced from the basement and was standing in the kitchen behind me. The shadow he casted manifested its way across the room and over top of me. I could feel the immediate chill of being underneath his presence.

With a flap of the shoe still lodged within my mouth, I slowly turned my head. My eyes were open widely and it only took me a moment of shifting my head until Sam was in center site of my peripheral vision. Just as my eyes captured the outer edge of Sam's dark silhouette, I dropped what was left of the mangled, soggy leather. Before my brain had time to process his lunge towards me, his booted foot was down on my face. I squealed like a fool and rammed up against the wall, trying to helplessly retreat.

As I fell to my side, I could see his face. Bitter and enraged, Sam kicked me in the snout two more times before yelling something I did not understand. The pain and blood on my face was interfering with my other senses, but Sam's wrath was short and over quickly- something I was grateful for.

Filled with soreness and shame, I slept there on the floor that night. Instead of sleeping in his bed, Sam slumbered on the couch with the television on. I couldn't confirm if he actually slept or not as I stayed on the floor in the kitchen surrounded by a bed of shredded leather and blood.

Chapter 3

Hot Cocoa

The next morning, after cleaning up my mess from the night prior, Sam left for work. That meant I was again back to being left home and alone. I spent most of my time on the couch drifting in and out of consciousness as I watched television. Sam had left it on for me, which was a treat he sometimes awarded as a distraction to keep me out of trouble. It was odd, though, to be in the middle of watching a movie only to have the picture cut away to someone who was not in the film so that they could inform me about a product that I was supposed to buy. These small breaks were almost hypnotizing in their presentation and often in their occurrence. It was really strange and left me wondering if something was wrong with Sam's television.

After napping my day away, Sam was home. I rushed to the door at the sound of his truck pulling into the driveway and watched as he strolled up the walkway. He was carrying a brown bag from the supermarket. He fiddled with his keys to unlock and open the door while juggling the goods, which was kind of funny to see. Once inside, he placed the bag down on the kitchen counter and ran off to the shower.

Not even so much as a hello.

Sam was in the bathroom for far longer than usual. The sound of the water running reminded me of how badly I had to pee, so I propped up against the front door and waited. When Sam came out of the bathroom, he was dressed in a collared shirt and a black pair of tight-fitting skinny pants. He was clean-shaven with his hair slicked back and looking shiny.

"You gotta go out?" he asked me as he plucked fine strands of destitute hairs from his shirt.

Yes, I do.

Sam walked over and opened the door for me. I was thrown off by Sam's current smell; it was overwhelmingly artificial and musky. If I had closed my eyes, I am not very sure I would even have known it were him that was near.

Heading outside and down the stairs of the porch, the evening air was crisp and refreshing. I found a good place to take a leak and then wandered around the yard for a bit while waiting for Sam to call me back in. I found a pile at the edge of the yard of a strange smelling bacterium. They were thin, white strands of squiggly vegetation with fat round caps for heads. I bit into them and chewed the stringy, fibrous plants. They tasted strange and not very appealing, but I swallowed them anyway.

Sam opened the door and I rushed into the house before he had the chance to summon me.

I am such a good dog.

"Alright Linus, I won't be back 'till pretty late, so be good."

Oh... Okay.

"Do you wanna watch TV?"

He walked into the living room and turned on the television, but my eyes just stared at him, pleading for some attention. He grabbed a jacket from out of the closet. It was a nice one that I had never seen him wear before. After fitting it over his button-up shirt, he walked out of the house and locked the door behind himself.

I climbed up onto the couch and sat down with a sigh. It had begun raining outside, which was soothing and mesmerizing. Though not tired, I found myself falling asleep as I felt my body slowly sinking into the couch; that is, until loud, boisterous, cracks of lightning jolted me to my feet. The thunderous roars outside ramped up in their intensity until one violently struck down into the street and caused a bright flare of an explosion.

The power in the house went out and I bolted over to a window, which granted the only source of light into the room. It wasn't much. With the moon being slain by rain, clouds, and electric bolts that fired from the sky, I stood firmly in the darkness.

A flash outside quickly illuminated the room. Everything looked as though it were lit up in the day time. Standing across the room was a woman. She was drenched in blood and covered from head to toe in open wounds. Maggots were squirming in her open, rotting skin. Her face was pale and emotionless. As my eyes dilated in fixation, the room again went dark. The transition felt like the walls all around me were melting inwards, and the delayed cracking sound of the lightning locked me into a firm stance.

That girl was not really there, right? It's just shadows at play in the dark.

Another flash of lightning lit up the room and my suspicion was confirmed; the girl was gone, but this time there was a dog. I had trouble remembering what my mother looked like, but something suggested that whoever this unknown canine was, somehow it was her. She was an old dog with long, dark hair and was laying on the ground. She was alive, but injured and not moving.

The room went dark, but I could still see the silhouette of the dog. The rain pelted against the window. I flinched and blinked as the sounds of madness descended upon the house. My eyes tried to again fixate on the injured dog across the room, but hovering over her was a man. A flash of light from another lightning bolt confirmed he was there. He had a long knife in his hands and he was hailing it down onto the injured dog. Again and again the man, with his back to me, plunged his blade into the canine, who lay still, accepting her fate. Her eyes were locked onto mine with a look of sadness, and the butchery continued as the room again fell dark.

More lightning strobed the room in light and my stomach churned in pain as the man turned to face me. He was covered in the dog's blood. Her entrails were wrapped around his hands and arms. He raised the blade he was holding in his hand up to his mouth. Sticking his tongue out, he licked the blade and sliced his tongue clean off. Blood oozed from his face while he smiled. Although he was covered in gore, I could still make the man out to be Sam. I pitched forward and vomited chunks of white and brown onto the floor.

The room flashed once more and everything I had seen was gone, as if it had never actually happened. I silently stood in place trembling for a few minutes in a state of shock. The sound of my urine hitting the hardwood floor was drowned out by the heavy rain that torrented the house. I bolted for the laundry room as another flash of light lit up the living room, revealing blood all over the walls. I could again see Sam. He was cutting up the dead dog's corpse with his blade. I buried myself in a pile of clothes as to not witness the scene any longer. The clothes felt like they were moving. It was creepy, but also warm and comforting though, so served to be a far better fate than what I was subjected to in the living room. I spent the rest of my night buried in the clothes, trying to think happy thoughts as I blindly listened to the sloshing sounds of shadow Sam butchering the dead dog while the storm wreaked havoc on the house.

The next morning, I lingered out of my hiding spot to meet Sam in the kitchen for breakfast. To my own surprise, I felt fantastic. The urine and vomit in the living room were cleaned up and Sam had not mentioned having come home at some point to find and attend to my mistake- something I was grateful for. The night before, my mind had played tricks on me and I felt foolish for being such a scared little pup amidst a measly rain storm. The images I had seen still terrified me. I knew that it all was over, but those images ended up vividly sticking with me for the rest of my life. After eating breakfast, Sam compiled a collection of tools and strapped his boots on.

"Gonna spend the day working outside. Do you wanna help?"

Yes!

Sam's upbeat mood was contagious and I rushed over to the door to join him on the adventure. I braced myself for the blast of frigid air as Sam opened the door, but it never came. The temperature outdoors was cold but tolerable. Green grass had laid claim over most of the yard and only faint pools of snow still lingered. I couldn't believe it. The snow was melting and winter was literally dissolving away into spring. I sprung forth out of the door and ran through the yard, being sure to pounce on every little white puddle that I could find. All winter long the snow had overpowered me with its vastness, but now, now I could dissolve the stuff simply by pressing a paw to it.

Sam measured out and cut up strips wood which he then placed up against the windows of the basement. One by one, he nailed the planks firmly into place. Aside from a meager glance, or two, I didn't pay him much mind. I was way too preoccupied with stamping out every last bit of winter I could find so that spring may feel welcome in her arrival.

I heard chirping coming from a row of soggy bushes

nearby, so I ran over and poked my head in to investigate. I found a bird who was alone and crying. It was strange to see one with no feathers. It seemed like some creepy little alien monster, but that's just how baby birds are born, I guessed.

Sam noticed the chirping in the bushes, which was now getting louder in response to me being there. He stopped what he was doing and arrived our way.

"What is it, Linus?"

I backed away and looked up to Sam to allow him access to the baby bird. Sam knelt down and inspected it, then picked it up with his gloved hands. He looked into the bird's chirping little face, then smiled. He glanced above us into a maple tree and then gently placed the bird in his front pocket. He reached up for a thick branch and pulled himself up with ease. Sam always was quite fit and athletic. He scanned through the leafless branches until he found what he was looking for: it was a tiny nest made of mud, twigs, and grass. Keeping his balance up in the tree, Sam reached in his pocket, retrieved the bird, then placed it into the nest before climbing back down.

"Good job," Sam said as he ruffled the fur on the top of my head before returning to his woodworking.

I followed him over and sat in the mud to watch him build. He was done boarding up the windows and was now constructing a large wooden box. Using a shovel, he dug into the ground against the backside of the house, then planted the box into the dug-out hole.

"Do you like it?" Sam asked with a smile.

What is it?

It was a box big enough for me to lay inside, but it had no top, and he only buried enough of it into the ground so that it would sit firmly in place.

"We will plant flowers in it for spring," Sam concluded as he removed his gloves from his hands and brushed some dirt off from his shirt.

Oh, that makes sense, I guess.

Sam took a rough piece of sandpaper to the box and spent the mid-morning fine tuning the appearance of the flower bed. When he was satisfied with its layout, he broke out a bucket of paint and coated the box a dark blue. Curiosity led me to the drying paint where I hunched over to give it a whiff. It made me feel dizzy and I absorbed some of it onto the tip of my nose.

"Hey!" Sam bellowed firmly.

I bolted across the yard and away from the paint. I knew I wasn't really supposed to touch it, but I had anyway.

After going back inside, Sam gave me a bath, which I was not all too thrilled about receiving. It felt good to be clean and I spent the rest of the day beside the fireplace, drying off and licking my fur. Sam spent the afternoon cleaning the house. He played music through the speakers in the living room and sang to the tune while attending to every bit of dirt and grime that lingered throughout the house.

When Sam was done cleaning, he put away his stuff and lit some candles in the house. They smelled like Christmas, which was weird given they were just sticks of melting wax. Sam went into the kitchen and began cooking something with onions.

I hate the smell of onions. Why would you cook onions after cleaning the house?

A knock on the door suggested that someone was here, but I was too preoccupied cleaning myself to check and see who it was. Sam answered the door and let whoever it was inside. I caught a waft of the scent of a familiar woman, then Natalie perked her pretty face around the corner from the kitchen.

"Hey, Linus," she cheered. "Long time no see!"

Though I was still uncomfortably soggy, I lifted myself up and ventured over to greet her with a wagging tail.

Hey, Natalie! How have you been?

"Oh, you're all wet," she pointed out as she ran her fingers through my fur.

"Yeah, he just had a bath," Sam defended.

Natalie took her coat off and sat down at the table where her and Sam talked for a bit while I re-attended to cleaning my fur. The two of them ate their stinky onion-based dinner, then joined me in the living room.

I am finally dry and my fur looks awesome!

Sam fixed a teapot onto some hinges that hung directly over the flames of the cozy fireplace, then he sat down beside Natalie on the couch. They talked about sailboats for a while. Apparently, Natalie's father had lived on one for most of his adult life and it was something that Mia was very passionate about.

My ears perked up as I flinched to the sound of a high pitched whistle, which screeched and screamed through my head. *What is that?*

"Awe. It's okay Linus," Natalie comforted with a pat on my head. "It's just the teapot."

Sam jumped up from the couch. Using a mitten, he carefully withdrew the squealing metal container from the open flame.

"I think it's cute," Natalie said, still rubbing the top of my head, "That you had the idea to boil the water over the open flame. It would be quicker to do on the stovetop, but it's far more romantic by the heat of the fire."

"Yeah, well... that's me, you know?" Sam said with a smile.

"No, I *don't* know... and that's what is so scary about all of this."

"How do you figure?"

"Well, I mean I only just met you. Yet I feel so comfortable around you after only our second date."

Sam churned his smirk into a more devious sort of smile as he placed a hand onto Natalie's shoulder. "Grab your cup and hold it out."

I guess he really does like her. Shawna is missing out,

wherever she is.

Natalie leaned forward, picked up her cup and held it out. "Careful."

"Of course," Sam said while reaching down to grab the stereo remote. "This is my favorite part," he added as he turned the music up as high as it would go. He closed his eyes and swayed his head back and forth to the melody of the tune. Then, with a grin, he opened his eyes and, missing the cup she was holding entirely, he poured the scalding hot water all over her fingers. Though outweighed by the boisterous music playing in the background, I could still hear Natalie's scream as she dropped her mug of powdered cocoa to the floor. The look on her face was one of tremendous agony as she pulled her hands in close to her chest and fell back on the couch.

With the music so loud, I found it hard to think. The entire house vibrated with the sounds of an eerie sort of epic opera.

Lowering his eyebrows, Sam discarded the empty teapot off to the side and backpedaled to the fireplace with a smirk and a scowl still on his face. Using a set of metal tongs, he withdrew a burning ember and approached Natalie. She was too busy looking at and cradling her burnt hands to notice him. He pressed the red ember against her already burnt hands. Again she screamed and again her cries were drowned out by the symphony of sound that claimed the house as its own.

Trying to escape, Natalie slumped off the couch and onto the floor. Sam scraped the burning ember up against her stomach. The glowing coal quickly burnt through her clothes and into her skin. As she screamed and struggled, Sam released the ember, then swung at Natalie's chest. After taking a blow with the metal tongs, she tried to defend herself with her charred hands. Sam didn't seem to care. He beat in her hands without hesitation just as he had done her chest.

With a mucus-filled cry, Natalie pleaded with Sam, who dropped the metal tongs and came down to meet her at eye level.

"Don't worry," he yelled over the music with a grin that stretched from cheek to cheek. "I won't hurt that beautiful face. I need it just the way it is."

Sam reached behind the couch and picked up a hatchet. *Was that always there?* He grabbed Natalie by her ponytail and pulled her head back. He pressed the hatchet up against her throat, then raised it high up in the air. With all of his might, he brought it down and into her neck. It dug deep and blood splattered in all directions. The room was caked in red. Some of the droplets got on my freshly cleaned coat and into my eyes. I flinched but continued to watch as, again and again, he hacked away at her neck. She had choked out the rest of her life on her own blood at some point between the first swing of his hatchet and the last.

He pulled at her head. Veins and arteries split apart, spewing blood in all directions as what was left of her neck broke away. The headless body slumped down to the floor and continued spritzing the ground with blood. With his left hand, Sam raised Natalie's decapitated head up to his face. Using his free fingers, he scrunched up her lips and pressed them to his. With blood all over himself, he reached for the stereo remote and brought the level of sound down to a tolerable level. He then took Natalie's head with him as he disappeared down into the basement for the rest of the night.

I was alone in the living room with Natalie's dead body which was lying on the floor in a pool of blood. My love for Sam was unyielding, but I felt angry. I was angry at him for ruining something so pure, beautiful, and innocent. I was angry at her for falling in love with him so quickly, and I was angry with myself for allowing it all to happen. It was an emotion that I had never really felt before, but with blood in my eyes, fur, and mouth, I too felt the urge to ruin something. I wanted to break something. I wanted to kill something.

Leaving the body in the living room, I went over to the door in the kitchen where Sam's shoes were neatly organized in a row. A pair of black leather heels, once belonging to Natalie, were off and to the side of the rack of shoes. I smelled them for a second and hesitated, contemplating if Sam would care. *Why would he?*

I ripped away chunks of leather from the heels. I gnawed on the pieces until my gums bled and the leather strips of the shoes were soft and gooey with saliva. I continued shredding the shoes into heaps of useless soggy scraps until nothing was any longer recognizable. With a large flap in my mouth, I shook my head back and forth like a maniac before dropping and collecting more to shake as violently as I could.

I hate you.

Chapter 4

Curiosity

Sam stayed awake that night. Sawing and drilling away in the basement, he continued his work through the wee hours of the AM and skipped out on going to work the next day. He spent his time home scrubbing the house down with chemicals and attending to the hardwood floors with a fresh coat of paint. He had rolled Natalie's body up into a thick plastic cocoon and dragged the disguised corpse out to the back yard where he heaved it into the large empty flower box that we had constructed days prior. He covered the body with bags of compost and dirt, then planted pretty flowers of orange and red over top of her. It was a raised plant box that served to conceal Natalie's corpse and lay her to rest amongst a bed of flowers. Fitting. She was a beautiful girl.

A few dull days went by until an eerie evening came into fruition. Sam was lying back on the couch and scribbling into a notebook. From time to time, he would undergo these artistic spells where he would succumb to an extended period of drawing.

I sat by his side, watching the embers in the fireplace as they danced the night away in the company of one another. At times, they would cackle, flare, and pop; discrepancies in their otherwise peaceful accord.

Just as my mind began to trip out from under the realm of understanding, the grandfather clock in the living room sounded off three times. Essentially, the big clock had suggested that the hour was well past midnight and morning was fast approaching.

Sam fell asleep on the couch and his notebook fell to the floor with a thud. I lifted my eyes from the ground before me to clearly see the page that the book had fallen open to. The page, though white by nature, was scribbled in a hateful sort of black. In the shadows of anger were patterns of madness. Screams and echoes of chaos bled through the paper via ink that was scratched in with such ferocity that it radiated from the book. Never in my life have I seen such an inanimate object glow with such hate. For some unknown reason, the imagery was so intense that I found I had to take leave from the room.

Heading out into the kitchen, I found a warm spot on the floor underneath the table. As I too drifted off to sleep, I could have sworn that I heard the cries and screams of a young girl of in the distance.

The next morning, I opened my eyes as my ears detected the sound of Sam's cell phone vibrating across the table above me. The sun was out and peaking its way through the glass door in the kitchen, which suggested that the morning was late and pressing into the afternoon.

Sam entered the room, picked up his cell phone, looked at it for a second, then set it back down on the table before leaving the kitchen to take his morning leak. The sound of him peeing in the bathroom reminded me that I too had to go pee, so I drowsily walked over to the door and sat down like a good dog to show Sam that I had to go outside.

The sound of footsteps sloshing through the wet yard captured my attention and I turned to look out of the window. I witnessed two men making their way up the path that led across the yard to the porch. Both men were well dressed. The one in the lead had black hair atop a clean-shaven, angry-looking face. He was tall and thick with a muscular sort of build that his trench coat did little to disguise. Behind him was the second man; who was also fit, but much skinnier. He had brown hair and a prickly-looking unshaven face that was far more welcoming and friendly in appearance than the angry mug of the leadman.

The larger man knocked on the door three times then turned to face his friend. I backed away as Sam zipped up the fly of his pants then approached and opened the door.

"Afternoon," said the hefty fellow. "Sam?"

"Yes," Sam admitted after a brief moment of hesitation.

"Samuel Isaiah Martin?" the sizeable stranger continued.

"Yes. What is this?"

"Well, Sam, I am Detective Steven Lugardo," the large man said. He raised his hand and flashed a shiny badge to accent his introduction of self. He then extended his arm toward the skinnier man that accompanied him. "And this is my partner, Detective Kyle Limon. Kyle and I are going around gathering some information on a missing person. We were wondering if we could trouble you for five minutes of your time with some questions?"

Sam, with an empty slate of emotion on his face, stared at the large man. His eyes then slowly drifted over to the skinnier one, whose own eyes were cold and still as he maintained an awkwardly engaged stare with Sam.

"Yeah. Sure," Sam said at last.

"Excellent. May we come in?" the husky fella pressed. "It's rather cold out today and I'm afraid my lanky friend here doesn't fare too well with the cold. Grew up in Tampa, this one, and is constantly bitching about our hearty northern winters. You'd think he would get used to it after being here for three years, but every day I have to listen to him whine about it."

The second detective, Kyle, lowered his eyebrows and faked a shiver in a way as if to mock himself.

"I have some things that need to be attended to, so can we make this quick?" Sam defended.

"Absolutely, Mr. Martin. As I said, this will only take a few minutes."

Sam propped the door open further and gestured the two men inside.

The larger man, Steven, walked in, glanced at me, and then began meticulously scanning the interior of the home. His partner, Kyle, followed in behind him and simply looked at me with a smile.

Sam's cell phone buzzed like a bee, yet again, across the kitchen table.

"Do you want to get that? You can," Steven suggested.

"No. It's fine. They will call back." Sam eased.

The skinnier man, Kyle, folded his arms and leaned up against the frame of the doorway that led into the dining room while his larger companion continued his observations.

"So, what's going on? Who are you guys searching for?" Sam questioned.

"Psh, some stupid girl who went missing a week ago. I keep saying that she is probably just off on a bender," Kyle said with a smirk. I couldn't shake the feeling that his tone was dripping with a sense of artificial sass. An overall fakeness- as if he were acting out the role of the good cop in one of those old police action flicks.

"Though Kyle and I differ in our beliefs on many fronts," the larger detective said as he turned to face Sam, "there is one thing both Kyle here and I share a passion for, and that's coffee. You like coffee, Mr. Martin?"

"Yeah. Sure. Occasionally," Sam admitted.

"*Occasionally*? Jeez, you hear that, Kyle? Sam only likes coffee occasionally. I didn't know anyone could drink coffee in moderation. Shit's as close to being a legal cocaine as there is in this world, and me, well, I just cannot seem to get enough of the stuff."

A silence fell over the room for a brief moment where both men seemed to read Sam like a book.

"Natalie Milano," the larger detective continued. "Girl that works at a coffee shop downtown is the chica we are tracking down. Word is you knew her?"

I could feel Sam's heart thumping out of his chest from across the room.

"Yeah I knew her... Sort of."

"Sort of?" the hefty detective pressed.

"We went on a couple of dates."

Looking relaxed with his arms still folded, the smaller detective uttered a phrase that stopped the beating of Sam's heart. "Phone records show you as being the last person to speak to her."

"Is that so?" Sam questioned with a blank face.

Unfolding his arms, Detective Kyle pulled a notepad from his back pocket and flipped through the pages. "Looks like she sent you a text message last Friday at about six p.m. that read, 'Running a little late. Be there in fifteen.' You remember seeing her last Friday, Mr. Martin?"

"Yeah. She came over for dinner. Was our second or third date. I haven't heard from her since she left that night."

"She didn't sleep over that night?" the larger man mocked as he turned to his partner. "I know they don't put out on the first date, but the third, I mean come on, am I right?"

"No, we had dinner, talked for a bit, had some hot chocolate, then she left. Said she had to work early."

Sam, I think that you are confusing 'her leaving' for you having decapitated her.

"You mean to tell me that you saw this girl under romantic circumstances on three separate occasions and then never heard from her again?" Steven pressed.

"Man, what went wrong?" Kyle interjected, again crossing his arms.

"Nothing. We had a nice time."

"Yeah, but to not hear from her again afterwards; didn't you begin to wonder why?

"I just figured she was busy."

"You two have an argument that night?" the larger man's question felt more like a suggestion that he backed up with his sharp, piercing eyes.

"Are you implying that I did something to her?"

"Implying that you did something to her? No, I didn't imply that. Did I, Kyle?" he added, turning to face his partner.

"No, I don't think that you implied that at all."

Turning back to face Sam, the larger detective squinted his eyes. "Sounded to me like *you* implied that you may have done something to her."

Suddenly fueled with a boost of confidence, Sam let loose. "Listen, you said that you wanted to ask me a few questions, not try to mind fuck me into some crackpot conspiracy. If I'm not under arrest, which clearly I am not- I've done nothing wrong- then I would like for you two to leave my house."

The larger man smirked. "I see," he said as he turned to take leave. "Well, Kyle. Looks like we are no longer welcome."

Kyle unfolded his arms and followed his partner out the door. "Damn, Sam. Your sister was a much better host. She even offered us a glass of milk while we chatted it up. I politely declined, of course. I find that stuff to be disgusting, really. I mean a cow's breast milk is intended for its child, you know? At what point in history did man decide that it would be a good idea to extract and consume the milk of another mammal? Yuck... Ole' tubs here though, you know he had himself two full glasses."

Now on the porch, the larger detective turned back so that he could bid us farewell. "Did Natalie tell you that she was three months pregnant, Mr. Martin?"

"What?" Sam said, wrinkling up his face.

"Maybe that's why she left," he added. "Went off to seek out ole' Dr. Kevorkian."

Sam said nothing. He closed the door and watched as the two men made their way across the lawn. I scurried to the front-most window of the house and listened to the two as they left.

"You do realize Dr. Kevorkian was a euthanization activist and not some crazed abortion doctor, right?" the younger detective, Kyle, mocked.

"What difference does it make? He got the gist," the muscled detective defended as he opened the passenger door to their car, which was parked out on the street. He turned back to glance over the house one last time before he dipped his head in and closed the vehicle's door.

After the two of them drove off, I went back out to the kitchen where Sam was blankly staring out the window. After a minute or two of the awkward silence, he noticed I was near and watching him.

"The hell are you looking at," Sam mumbled. He took off for the basement with a sigh.

I laid myself down next to the door and placed my head flush against the kitchen tile floor.

That was intense.

Sam's cell phone rattled across the table once more. Despite it buzzing on and off all morning, I still flinched with the thought that its vibrations sounded like some giant monster of a bee swooping down to impale an intruder.

Just as the buzzing ceased, there were three bangs on the door behind me. I jumped and turned to see Sam's sister, Mia, pressing her face against the glass door before banging on it again three more times.

My tail began to wag uncontrollably as Mia jiggled the handle and the unlocked door popped right open. "Hey, Linus," she said as she stuck her head in through the cracked door.

Hi, Mia!

"Sam!" she yelled, her voice carrying its high pitched weight throughout the house as she entered.

I think he is in the basement.

"What are you doing just walking into my house?" Sam growled as he surfaced from the basement and slammed the door closed behind himself.

Both Mia and I flinched, startled by his presence.

"Why do you never answer your phone, Sam? I have been trying to call you all morning."

While keeping his posture straight and his stance firm, he stood guard in front of the basement door. Sam's eyes slowly examined Mia and me. "So," he said calmly. "What did you tell them, Mia?"

"What do you mean? There is nothing to tell... Is there?" Mia countered. With a look of confusion on her face, she slowly scanned him up and down with her eyes.

"Do you think that I did something to her?" he questioned as he slowly moved away from the cellar door.

"What? No! That's ridiculous!" Mia defended.

"Then why are you here?"

"I was worried about you, Sam!"

"Why would you be worried about me if I have done nothing wrong?" he taunted.

"Sam... you're scaring me."

"Am I, Mia? *Why*? Why would *you* be afraid of *me*?"

"Because you're acting... insane."

Out of nowhere, Sam backhanded her in the face. Not expecting as such, she fell backwards and crashed into a shelf of herbs and spices. Raising her hand to comfort her now sore face, she glanced up to Sam, wearing an expression of pure hopelessness.

"*I* am the only one in our family who was *not* insane you stupid… fucking… *cunt!*"

The statement felt dangerously sharp as the words sliced across the room. I stepped in front of Mia and looked up to Sam, who had his eyes locked and swelling as they pierced through Mia like a blade.

Okay, Sam, enough.

"You hold our mother in such high regard, but last I checked *she* was the schizophrenic drug addict, not me. *She* was too busy shooting up while I was taking care of *you!*"

Mia's face began to twitch as tears took to a ready position.

"Move, Linus," Sam said, seething through the teeth of his clenched jaw.

Please, Sam, relax. Let Mia go. Please.

Glancing down at me, Sam twitched his upper lip. "*Move,*" he growled.

No, Sam. You need to calm down. Please. Please stop it!

With the power of a thousand and one trampling horses, Sam's concrete fist came crashing down across my face. What a naive fool I was to think that I could stand between his wrath and the target he was honed in on. Collapsing to the floor like a cardboard box in a hurricane's path, I could taste the blood that quickly filled my mouth. In falling, I must have bitten my tongue.

"Sam! Stop it!" Mia screamed.

Stop he would not. Disoriented, I looked up to the source of shadow that was cast down upon me. Sam was standing directly overhead. Dropping to his knees with a clenched jaw and tightened fist, he unleashed his anger. His eyes boiled with hatred as he wailed on me again and again and again.

Squealing out in pain I squirmed to make way to somewhere safe. Using his left hand, Sam grabbed my collar and kept me pinned down while he continued bashing my sides in with his dominant right hand.

"Sam!" Mia again screamed as she crawled up behind me. She placed a soft hand on my side and raised another in the air to halt Sam's rampage.

Sam's chest was periodically rising and falling as he inhaled gusts of air.

"Fuck you, Mia," he said softly.

Though tensions were still high, the storm seemed to calm. Little did I know that I was in the eye of the storm, a calm moment just before more chaos ensues. Like a bolt of lightning, Sam loosened his grip on my collar and launched over top of me. All of his weight landed down on Mia. Pinning her to the ground, he swung at her face with more strength than I had ever seen a man possess.

Her squeaks and squeals were nothing compared to the sounds of his fists cracking the bones in her face. With all of the strength that she could muster, she fought back and tried to defend herself, but it was useless. With Sam on top of her and her hands pinned down by his knees, Mia looked so impotent.

After spending a few minutes tenderizing her face with all of his strength, Sam exhausted his reservoir of rage. He still sat atop of Mia's motionless body with his back to me. It was painful for me to try to move and see for sure, but the blood covering the floor suggested that he had done irreversible damage. Crawling my way forward, I moaned and cried out in agony.

Sam ignored me as he stood to his feet. He let out a sigh and turned to walk away. His face, shirt, and knuckles were drenched in blood. His stepping aside granted me the vision to fully see Mia. Though her eyes were open wide, she was not moving.

Sam went down into the basement. Despite my body being broken and bloody, I managed to get up and limp my way over to Mia. Her face was mangled badly with large open wounds that flooded forth blood like an undammed river. It didn't look like she was breathing. I placed my snout down against hers to feel if she was exhaling any air, but she was not. Her once pretty face was all but unrecognizable. The amount of severe lacerations that ran across the surface of her skin was so high, my stomach felt sick in trying to even begin to comprehend the extent of her damage.

Mia, get up. You have to get up and get out of here.

I licked some of the blood away from her wounds. The taste was awful, like metal, but I wasn't doing it for myself. For a split second, I thought that I could save her.

Please, Mia. Get up.

The red ink I smeared away with the tip of my nose revealed an even deeper collection of gashes and open, exposed meat. Mia's wounds slowly refilled with blood as I pulled away and observed.

"Move away, Linus," Sam said coldly from behind me.

I was startled by his presence and clumsily pulled back. Sam had resurfaced from the basement with a hacksaw and a tarp. Dropping both, he came down to my level and raised his hand to my face. I flinched.

I do not want to be hit anymore, Sam.

Sam rubbed his bloody fingers through the fur of my face. His hands slowly made their down my neck as he continued to softly scratch me.

"I am sorry," he whispered as his big blue eyes began to swell up and water.

I said nothing. I knew he was sorry. He had a darkness inside of himself that bled through his skin from the pits of his soul. It claimed control over his consciousness at times, but Sam was my friend. He was my family. He was the alpha male of our pack and I loved him.

Pulling me in tight, Sam buried his face into my fur and silently cried.

It's okay, Sam. It's okay.

Chapter 5

Bully

Sam spent the afternoon using his power tools to dismantle his dead sister into tiny little pieces- small enough to fit into black trash bags. The house was dark as all the shades were pulled tightly shut. I didn't want to be around to witness the work, but Sam would not let me go outside. Dressed in a lab coat, goggles, and gloves, he handled his business while I watched television in the living room. Sam had left the TV on for me and for that I was grateful. With the blade saw running every few minutes, it was hard to make out the words on the show, but the visuals were as good a distraction as ever. Keeping my mind away from the sound of the blade spinning as it tore through Mia's dead corpse was my utmost priority.

I endured a few hours of listening to Sam and his machines chop his sister up. The event was mentally draining and I was beginning to feel the physical fatigue of being sluggish and weak. How Sam could perform such a task with ease was a feat well beyond my grasp of understanding.

"Linus, you wanna go outside?" Sam echoed from around the corner.

Yes!

Finally, he was finished. I dashed out into the kitchen. Mia was gone and the floor was not only clean with a shine to it, but it also smelled of ammonia, which served to make me feel dizzy and woozy. Sam opened the door and, like an idiot, I slammed into the frame, missing the open exit entirely.

"What the hell?" Sam said, squinting down at me.

I am sorry, I got really dizzy there for a second.

I slowly limped out the door and Sam followed suit behind me, carrying two thick trash bags. They were black to conceal whatever may be inside. Given we typically use clear trash bags; I was left to assume that these ones were specifically chosen to conceal the identity of Mia within; or at least what was left of her.

I jumped down from the porch and stood aside so that Sam may pass by with his bags. He walked over to the truck and tossed them in the back of the empty bed.

"You want to go for a ride, Linus?" he asked as I was taking a leak on some bushes that smelled like a skunk. To not miss my opportunity at going for a ride, I nearly peed on myself as I ran over.

Sam opened the truck door. Without wasting any time, I jumped up and inside successfully. We pulled out of the driveway and ventured off. I wasn't sure where we were going, I was just grateful to be along for the journey. After a few minutes of travel, we had made it off of the main roads and into the backcountry. We took muddy backroads that were bumpy and fun to be riding down. In hitting one of the bumps, both Sam and I flew up into the air for a second with a good amount of clearance between our butts and seats that they sat in. Sam looked at me and laughed while rubbing my head with one hand and continuing to steer with the other.

With the two of us now on a narrow dirt road that was surrounded on both sides by an eerie forest of leafless trees, branches clawed away at the exterior of the truck. Their scrapes and snags against the hull of our ship frightened me, but Sam kept petting me. Though I was a coward, he was afraid of nothing.

We pulled into an opening that perhaps once served as a driveway. Sam turned the truck off and through the forest of dark trees I could see an old, abandoned house. Part of the building was caved in and some of the plant life had decided to lay claim over the fallen structure.

Sam climbed out of the truck and I followed close behind. "No, you stay here," he warned, turning to shut the door. *Right, okay.*

I didn't want to stay behind. There was a certain sort of darkness about this landscape that raised the hairs along my neck, but who was I to argue?

Sam reached for the two black trash bags in the back of the truck and set off through the brush towards the creepy looking house. Though I was stuck in the truck, I could hear his boots sloshing about in the mud. He veered off to the left and made way for what looked to be a quagmire. Just as his feet began sinking into the wet ground, he stopped and dropped both of the bags. He then picked up a stone and threw it ahead of him. The rock slowly sunk into the marsh. Sam picked up one of the bags and swung it around his body, to transfer momentum, before heaving it off into the swamp. He then did the same with the second bag. Sam closed his eyes and rolled his neck. He then reached inside his jacket pocket and pulled his pack of cigarettes out. He withdrew one of the sticks and lit it up, then he preceded to enjoy in the sullies of his addiction as he watched both trash bags, that were filled with the bits of his dead sister, sink off into the darkness.

***

As we pulled into the driveway, my suspicions of our journey being over before it had ever really started were confirmed. I had high hopes that our afternoon was to be an adventure, but it was okay. I was grateful to get out for a bit, nonetheless.

Our evening at home was quiet and dull. Sam sat in front of the fire scribbling on a pad with a pen while I sat hunched over on the couch watching television. I fell asleep at some point and woke up the next morning to the sound of someone pounding on our front door. I dashed to the entrance and, as usual, I made it there long before Sam. Our guest was a man wearing a black trench coat. He was a handsome fellow despite his messy, unkempt head of greasy brown hair and prickly, unshaven face. I noticed the man's eyes were sunken-in and bloodshot, which suggested he hadn't slept in a good bit.

Sam shirtlessly approached from the bathroom with shaving cream slathered across his face. He was getting ready for work just before the foreign man had shown up and began pounding on the door.

"What is up, Vince?" Sam questioned after unlocking and opening the door.

The fragrance of Mia and her home burst in through the entrance. That was when I realized that Vince was Mia's husband. Every time I had gone over there, he was only around briefly and not very often; I figured it was reasonable for me to have not recognized him. Though Sam was physically fit, Vince looked much bigger and stronger. Pushing his way through, Vince quickly placed his fingers around Sam's neck and slammed him against the wall.

"Where the fuck is she, you psycho?" he roared as he struggled to maintain his grip on Sam's neck with all of the foamy shaving cream slipping between his fingers.

Hey, stop it! I barked.

"Linus!" Sam yelled.

I don't understand, why would you not want my help? You are being attacked.

I stepped back and watched as Sam gave into Vince. The two locked eyes and Vince gritted his teeth while seething with anger.

"I don't know what you're talking about, Vince, but if you let me go we can talk like adults," Sam suggested as he struggled to breathe.

"You know exactly what I am talking about. Mia called me at work yesterday crying! Something about the cops coming to our house, *my house,* to ask questions about you murdering some chick? Then she said that she was going to go check in on you and I haven't heard from her since. She didn't call me back, she didn't pick up the kids from school, and she didn't come home last night."

Vince discarded Sam off to the side. Sam flew like a brick through the air and crashed into the kitchen table, the legs of which snapped and collapsed under his forced weight.

"I didn't see Mia yesterday, Vince. You are acting insane," Sam defended while gasping for air from being choked. "The cops came by looking for a girl that both *Mia* and I had seen a while back. After they left, Linus and I went on with the rest of our day, but my sister was not here."

Vince reached down and grabbed Sam by the hand. He lifted him to his feet, then pulled him in closely. "I never did like you. Something about you always rubbed me the wrong *goddamn* way. If I find out that you're lying," Vince warned calmly, "I will strangle you in your sleep."

"I am not lying," Sam reassured.

Vince quickly pitched his head forward and bashed Sam's face in before discarding him back into the broken bits of the table. He then looked around the room. His eyes locked into mine for a moment and, with a scowl, he left the house, slamming the door on his way out.

With blood dripping from his nose, Sam leaned back and sighed. I went to his side and licked his hand. He reached up and scratched my neck, but he did not get up.

"I guess I am not going to work today," he admitted with a mouthful of blood.

***

Sam cleaned up his face and took the bits of broken table out to the curb for disposal. Once back inside, he pulled all of the shades closed, which blocked out the sun and made the house seem as though it were night time.

Sam filled the bathtub full of bubbles and hot water. He then locked himself away inside the bathroom. This left me to myself once more.

My teeth and mouth felt sore. I had to chew on something- anything. But last time I ruined something of Sam's I got my ass kicked. In hindsight, chewing on Sam's shoes was a foolish puppy mistake. I should have gone for something he didn't really care about. Natalie's shoes were a good choice, but with her buried in the flower box out back, she wouldn't be coming along with a fresh pair of leather anytime soon.

I paced around the house and began to whine. My mouth really hurt. Then it dawned on me: *the wood on the backside of the couch! Sam never goes behind the couch and will never know.*

I spent the afternoon gnawing at the wood behind the couch while keeping an open ear out for Sam for when he finished with his warm bath. In time, there was a big gash in the wooden frame. I shouldn't have done it, but it felt so good on my teeth and gums. As soon as Sam exited the bathroom, I dashed into the kitchen and played dumb. He would never know what it was I had done.

A knock on the door startled me, and Sam peaked through the blinds to scout out who it was before cautiously answering.

"Jesus, man, what happened to your face?" a skinny guy dressed in a tie-dye tee shirt and blue jeans said as he pushed his way in. His face was narrow and clean cut with messy red hair covering the top of his head.

"I don't want to get into it, Nathan," Sam groaned. "What do you want?"

"You alright? You didn't show up for work today, or call, or anything."

"Yeah, I am fine," Sam eased half-heartedly.

"Cops came around the warehouse asking questions about you. Said they spoke with you yesterday. Did *they* do *that* to you?" the man, Nathan, asked as he gestured to Sam's broken face.

"No," Sam snickered. "What did they ask about? ... No, you know what? I don't even care."

"You are acting like the mafia is after you, man. I am on my lunch break, so I have a few minutes. Sit down and tell me what's going on."

"They might as well be," Sam sighed as he took a seat in a chair where the table used to be. "I just don't feel safe at home, is all."

Nathan glanced around into the darkness of our home, then he propped up against the wall in the kitchen and folded his arms. Looking down at Sam, he said "So what, the cops paid you a visit and now it's the end of the world? If I turned into a mopey little bitch every time those pigs gave me a hard time, I would be a makeup-wearing comatose vegetable."

"You would be wearing makeup?" Sam questioned as he squinted his eyes.

"Yeah, you know, like a goth kid." Nathan defended.

Sam turned his head down towards me and rolled his eyes. "You're a fucking idiot."

What did I do?

"You get the idea," Nathan said with a laugh. A moment

of silence fell over the room, then Nathan cleared his throat. "You didn't do it. Did you?"

"No," Sam said coldly while maintaining his gaze on the floor.

"OK then. What the hell are you worrying about?"

"They think I did it, Nathan, and when cops think someone did something, they don't usually let up until they find a way to frame the poor motherfucker."

"You're being crazy, man. Take a deep breath and relax."

"Was thinking about getting a shotgun," Sam said, raising his head so that he could look at Nathan and analyze his reaction.

"I support the hell out of the second amendment, but the last thing a scared guy living alone needs is a gun. Gonna end up shooting a hole through the wall when you jump at shadows in the night. Now if you want a little piece of mind, get a pitbull."

"A pitbull?" Sam challenged with offset eyebrows.

"Yeah. Great dogs. My cousin breeds and trains them for defensive purposes. God knows this bitch doesn't do anything to make you feel safe," Nathan said gesturing down to me. "A pit will, though."

Who you callin' a bitch? I am a male dog. And I can protect Sam just fine!

"Pitbulls are not born psychopathic serial killers. That's just Hollywood bullshit," Sam stated.

"Yeah, they can be sweet dogs, but there is a reason that they have been the dog of choice for fights and defense. Their physical build is where the potential lies. You train a hundred pounds of pure muscle to rip something apart, that something won't be recognizable given an hour. My cousin does just that. His pits cost a little more, but they are primed and ready for defense right out of the box."

"Right out of the box," Sam echoed back. "...Show me."

***

So that spring, a new addition to our home was acquired. In this corner, weighing in at just shy of a hundred pounds of pure muscle and strength: the black and white all-mean killing machine, Rex.

For the first few days that Rex was around, Sam spend a lot of time working with him one on one. I guess he had to get him accustomed to who the alpha male of our house was, a title Sam had no intentions of giving up easily. Meanwhile, I had spent that time locked away in the laundry room. I guess it was important that I did not intrude on their training sessions.

From the cracks under the door, I could see the shadows of both Sam and Rex as they sparred with one another. Fighting with each other seemed to be a hobby that the two of them shared in having.

I couldn't eat, drink, or go outside. I spent the entire day holding in the need to go pee while I listened to the two of them wrestle. As my bladder reached its breaking point, I stuck my nose as far under the door as I could get it and then began to whine.

"All right. No. *Sit*," Sam firmly instructed of Rex. Then, after Rex obliged, Sam came over to the door that I was locked behind and freed me.

Though I had seen Rex a few times, this was the first time he had seen me. His eyes burned with anger as he watched me exit the room. I quickly tucked my tail down between my legs and held my head low. I was not interested in conflict and I had to reflect that in my demeanor.

After going outside and taking a leak, I quickly re-entered the house and tried to introduce myself to Rex in a way that he would find respectable. As I turned the corner into the living room, Rex's burning, hateful eyes seared through my soul.

"On the couch, Linus," Sam instructed of me and, like the good boy that I was, I obliged to his command. I sat on the couch and watched Sam and Rex tire each other out playing and fighting on the ground until the time had come for the three of us to go to sleep for the night.

The next day was the first that I was home alone with Rex. Sam had spent the night prior keeping an eye on the two of us and how it was that we interacted with one another. For the most part, this meant I kept my distance while Rex sat, stood, and lay firmly where ever he saw fit. He made it clear within a matter of minutes that I was never to so much as approach him.

With Rex sleeping, I hopped down off of the couch to discover a stack of newly purchased toys in the corner of the living room. There were squeaky toys, a rubber kong, some thick pieces of knotted up rope, a few fake rubber bones that smelled of beef, and even some yellow tennis balls!

I picked up one of the tennis balls and began to wag my tail with excitement.

Sam never leaves these out for me to play with. They are one of my absolute favorite of things.

Like a puppy who had the opportunity to play with one for the very first time, I, now a much older dog, enjoyed in the fruits of the spoils as I gnawed on the tennis ball. *I bet I can fit two of them into my mouth.* Wasting no time, I reached down and tried to cram another into my mouth. *Ha, I did it! I wonder if I can fit a third into my mouth.* It wasn't easy. Every time I managed to snatch up a third ball, one of the other two would drop from my mouth. I laid myself down with my paws outstretched in front of me so that every time I dropped a ball it wouldn't get away. After a few minutes of fiddling with the balls, I managed to get all three into my mouth. I stood up triumphantly, but my moment of success was brief. Within seconds, I lost control and dropped all three balls. I managed to pin one down, then quickly jumped over to the second. After securing it against the ground, I leaped on top of the third. It bounced up and headed straight for Rex, who was still asleep at the other end of the room. Like a rug being pulled out from under me, my amusement vanished as the ball smacked down against Rex's snout.

I stood in place and watched in horror as Rex sprung up to his feet and glared at me from where he resided a few feet away.

He ramped up a light growl until his level of energy spilled over, then he snapped and barked at me like a maniac. Though his display of strength in that moment was but only a fraction of what he could muster, I felt like I was looking into the eyes of a storm, one so powerful that it could rain down from the heavens and claim over entire cities with ease.

Before he could attack, I bolted through the house and towards the bathroom outside of the kitchen. I knew Rex wouldn't go in there, as he disliked the feeling of the marble floor on his paws. It was perhaps the only safe zone in the house, but I had to get there first.

Foaming at the mouth like he had completely lost it, Rex drooled all over himself while running in pursuit after me. My only advantage was my speed and agility. If he caught me, he could kill me. I turned for the kitchen but lost my grip on the hardwood floor and smashed into the wall. Disoriented, I watched in slow motion as Rex drew near. Stumbling like some drunken fool, I clambered my way into the kitchen. Rex was directly behind me and I panicked, picking up speed as I turned towards the bathroom. I miscalculated my turn and slammed into the cellar door, which blew open, and through the air I tumbled down the stairs into the dank dark basement below.

Rolling to a dirty and dusty stop, I struggled to stand back up. Despite the boost of adrenaline granted to me from the chase, I felt as though I had possibly fractured something in my fall down the stairs. I pressed the thought of pain out of my mind and tried my best to ignore the taste of blood that quickly filled my mouth. I glanced up to the open door. Rex was staring down at me from the top of the stairs. He didn't come down. Despite being broken and in pain, in a way, I had at last caught a break.

Knowing I would likely have to stay down there until Sam got home, I looked around a bit. Most everything in the basement was meticulously up kept and stored away neatly. There was a work bench with strange metallic tools of various shapes and sizes. Some of the instruments were embedded into the table, while others simply hung overhead. Some were sharp and others blunt, but the thing in common that they all shared was just how clean, shiny, and evenly spaced out from one another they were.

To the right of the workbench was a sink large enough for even me to fit inside. Near that was a stack of loose bricks.

I caught a waft of something strange. It smelled like the frozen meat that Sam would get from the market from time to time. I spun around to notice the wall directly behind me was not like the others. Most of the walls were stone, but this one was wooden. The closer I limped over to it, the more I could distinguish it as the culprit that concealed a distinct scent of cold meat. My curiosity pleaded with me to investigate what exactly was behind the wall, but my fear denied me the freedom of inspection. Instead, I backed away as I heard, or so I thought I heard, the faint and muffled moanings of a girl coming from behind the wall.

The front door upstairs slammed shut and, with it, I flinched.

Sam was home.

It didn't take him long to notice the basement door was open and he appeared at the top of the steps with a look of caution while he held on tightly to a large kitchen knife.

"Linus," he said coldly, "What the *fuck* are you doing?"

I whined as I approached the first step of the staircase. It was all too painful to try to make it up onto even the lowest stair, let alone fathom working my way up and through the rest.

"Get up here," Sam resonated coarsely.

I tried to climb the first step, but my body simply would not allow it.

Sam slowly glided down the staircase with his eyes bulged and darting from side to side. Upon reaching me, he inspected the cellar before stuffing the knife in between his belt and his pants. He then reached down to pick me up. I squealed out in pain at being moved, but he ignored my cry as he carried me up the stairs. We walked past Rex, who eyed me like a stone gargoyle who was unmoved by much of anything. Sam set me down on the couch and then left for the basement.

Rex knew I was hurt. As long as I stayed on the couch and out of his way, he would leave me alone. So I did just that.

A few months passed and all was mostly quiet in our lives. Sam had stopped seeing women and, in time, the addition of Rex helped to ease his worries of security. I spent my days keeping my distance from Rex. Typically, this meant I slept in the bathroom from the time Sam left for work until the time he came home. The closest Rex and I had ever gotten to one another in that time was during meals. Our food dishes were a few feet apart and I had learned to eat as fast as I could, because when Rex was done with his meal, he would move onto mine. Without so much as a look in my direction, he stuck his face into my dish and devoured what was left of my food. Steering clear of all conflict, I accepted this as the norm.

A few nights later, I awoke from where I slept in the bathroom. Knowing that it was time for dinner, I exited the bathroom and entered the living room where Sam was on the ground with a set of weights, working out.

"Get out of here, boy," Sam chuckled as Rex appeared hovering over top of him.

Rex did not move. It was time for dinner and the beast was hungry.

"I am going to kick your fucking ass if you don't move," Sam warned in a joking manner.

Still, the monster didn't move and Sam, acting on his warning, reached up and pinned the barbaric dog to the ground with ease. Rex shifted into fight mode. Though scaled back to a level of play, his ferocity was unmatched by anyone I had ever seen. He and Sam struggled on the ground, wrestling and pinning one another for a few minutes before Sam got a good hold on Rex's neck. Sam shifted his body weight down onto the dog and firmly held him in place. Then, with hoarseness in his voice, he leaned in and whispered into Rex's ear, "You lose." Sam stood back up and released the maniac, who was quick to try for a rebuttal. "Alright," Sam added, breathing heavily. "Go play with your toys."

Rex walked away unscathed from the trial by combat. He went over to the corner, where a pile of his broken toys lay. He grabbed one that used to squeak like a duck. There wasn't much left to the ball of slobber and shredded cloth, but he went on to shake it about like a dead carcass that he intended to devour anyway. The intensity in which he mangled his toys reminded me of just how powerful he was. Though Sam could beat Rex in a fight, Rex could kill Sam if he really wanted to. Though, to be fair, I suppose Sam could just as easily murder Rex if he really wanted to, as well. I stared on as Rex caused destruction with his toys. As much as I hated him, there was no denying that Rex was built to be a weapon of war. *I wonder what it was like for his mother to have had to give birth to such a monster.*

I went into the kitchen and sat down by the refrigerator, which was directly across the room from my food dish. It was dinner time, but Sam was busy.

No worries. Just a little late, is all, I thought while resting my head to the ground and closing my eyes.

Just as soon as my vision was dark, I felt the presence of the house demon enter the room. I was afraid to open my eyes, and instead played as though I were asleep in hopes that he would just leave me alone. I heard him gather his bowl with the orifice of his mouth. It cracked under the weight of his jaw as he clenched down on to it. I broke the agreement that I had made with myself to not look. I slowly peeked one eye open and then the other. The great God of a beast was angry for the lack of offerings made to him. He was shredding his plastic dish and tossing the ripped pieces aside as if they were nothing but feathers to a pillow.

When the bits of the shredded dish were scattered across the floor, he concluded his fit of maiming and turned to face me. Again, I clenched my eyes shut in hopes that he would not target me with his rage. I could hear him slowly walk over to my bowl and stop.

Please don't rip up my food dish, too.

Before he had time to destroy my container, Sam entered the room and I opened my eyes.

"I know it's dinner time, but come the fuck on, guys," he complained as he looked over the room, which was covered in shredded bits of plastic.

I didn't do anything...

Sam reached down to my food dish, which had survived through Rex's onslaught of his own. "Looks like you two will have to share for now," Sam explained as he filled up my bowl and placed it on the ground. To compensate for there being only one dish, he graciously filled it to the brim and Rex didn't waste a second diving into the food. "Don't eat it all, Rex, save some for Linus," Sam added as he went into the bathroom and stripped off his sweaty clothes so that he could take a shower.

I don't know whether Rex hadn't heard Sam or whether he had and chose not to care, but his face was buried in the mound of food and he showed no signs of including me in his dinner plans. If I wanted Rex to share our meal with me, I would have to assert myself and let him know of my desire. I advanced forward, but as soon as Rex sensed me moving behind him, he paused his inhalation of dinner and growled, keeping his face buried in the dish.

Okay, I get it. I will just wait.

I took a seat and did just that. When Rex was sated and full, he left the room. I scurried over to the dish where I found that he had saved me some of the food. I dug right in. I didn't care that the bits were caked in Rex's slobber or that I had to wait and eat second. I was just grateful to be eating dinner.

The next morning, I was not so lucky as to be saved any of breakfast. Sam left for a day of work and that meant I was forced to spend the day keeping clear out of Rex's sight and counting the sands of time as I waited for Sam to again come home.

Laying in the bathroom up against the toilet, I felt my stomach growl. The sounds it made echoed across the cold, hard floor and I did my best to try and think of something, anything, that would disguise my hunger from my mind. Every minute that passed felt like days that would never end. When the sun would set on one day, the heinous night would follow in suit, forcing me to dwell on dark thoughts that I would rather not recollect. This cycle lasted in a rinse and repeat fashion for a time so protracted in its repetition that I could feel myself slipping slowly into the warm embrace of insanity.

By the time Sam was supposed to come home and dinner be served, I didn't bother to get up from the floor and wait. There was no point. It got to the point where I could have stood by the door like I did every day prior and greet my loving master, but I felt weak and alone; so instead I closed my eyes and slept.

I awoke to the sound of the front door opening later on in the night. I was unsure of how late it was, but with a thick moon peeking in through the window of the bathroom, I was left to assume it was well past midnight. I poked my head out of the bathroom to see Sam entering in through the front door of the house. To say that he was coming home unusually late would be putting it lightly. He was dragging a girl inside who was slouched against him as he held her arm tightly around his shoulder. She had an oddly-shaped face. With skin so smooth it may have very well been made of silk and honey, she had black hair and funny looking slanted eyes. No doubt that, despite her abnormal appearance, she was gorgeous. Maybe she was even the prettiest girl Sam had ever been with. Though her eyes were closed, I could see the essence of life radiate from the girl, and because of this I knew that she was alive.

Perhaps she is asleep.

"What?" Sam asked me while Rex entered the room and sat down to join in watching the spectacle with our house guest unfold.

With a sigh, Sam set the girl down in a chair and picked up our food dish. After filling it to the brim, he slid it across the floor towards us, then lifted the girl from the chair and dragged her down into the basement.

The moment he was out of sight, I looked to Rex. He didn't bother to look back and dove straight into the bowl of food. He was relentless. I slowly moved forward and dipped my head low. I wouldn't forcefully push my snout into the dish to share the meal with him- to do so would be foolish. I had decided that I would wait for him to pull back with a mouthful and then, while he was chewing, I would snag a mouthful for myself. Rex tensed up and lowered his shoulders as I drew near. He had no intentions of sharing the meal, as per usual, and as I entered into his comfort zone within a biting reach, he lifted his face. Snapping and snarling, he caught me on the neck. I quickly tried to squirm out from under him, but his jaw snapped down on the top of my head, just between both of my eyes. His teeth sunk into my skin. Though I screamed and tried to pull out the rest of the way, he had latched on with his steel-like jaw. Rex gave off a vicious growl while shaking me back and forth like some chew toy before discarding me off to the side like unwanted pieces of scrap.

I ran off to the living room and sat upright behind the couch. I could smell the blood that dripped down my face. It hurt badly and I could hear the droplets pool down onto the floor below me, but in that moment, I was just grateful to be alive. I had lost my appetite and now I just had to focus my attention on staying away from that maniac. As soon as he was finished devouring his meal, Rex exited the kitchen and entered the living room. I slowly peeked an eye out from behind the couch. I let out a whine when Rex licked his lips and stared at me with his devious expression of madness. I pulled my face back in behind the couch so as to not look him directly in the eyes and then I painfully squeezed my own eyes tightly closed.

Maybe if I ignore him he will leave me alone.

I heard a pillow slide off the couch, followed by the sound of Rex growling and shredding the fluffy ball of thread and cotton. I figured then would be a good time to run out of the room, so I sprang forth. As soon as I had moved out from behind the couch, I was in Rex's line of sight. He dropped the pillow and tackled me to the ground. Keeping me pinned down, he growled and dripped saliva onto my bloody face. As soon as I let out a cry and flinched, he sunk his teeth into my neck and kept me locked down against the ground. With such a firm grip on my throat, I was left gasping for air. His level of intensity and energy was hellish. It made the encounter feel as though I were facing off against the wrath of God in some unholy demonic form and all the weight of the very elements that he commanded. Then, out of nowhere, he loosened his grip and allowed me the opportunity to get up. Rex watched me very carefully as I left the room, crying and bleeding. This was as clear a warning as ever, to stay away from Rex *always* and at *all costs.*

A high pitched scream echoed up from the basement below. The girl Sam had brought home was awake and in agony. I passed by the steel food dish in the kitchen. Despite not being hungry any longer, I glanced down at it. It was empty. The screams from below the wooden floors of the house intensified. The girl was dying, slowly and painfully.

I went into the bathroom and laid my head down beside the cold basin of the porcelain toilet. Sleeping was about all that I was allowed to do in my own house.

Chapter 6

Acceptance

A few nights later, while Rex and I were home alone, Sam slammed up against the glass door of the house. Rex quickly shifted into a defensive stance. It was dark outside, which made it hard to see what exactly was going on. A moment later, Sam disappeared into the unknown and then again slammed up against the window.

Was someone hurting him?

The door handle rattled and the sound of Sam's keys jingling could be heard as he entered the house. Someone was with him, and Rex sprung into attack mode.

"Go lay down," Sam sternly instructed of Rex. Being the obedient little monster that he was, Rex obliged and moved away from the door.

As Sam entered, he was accompanied by a skinny,

blonde-haired girl. Her arm was slung over his shoulder and he was struggling to escort her inside. As they stumbled their way in, Sam used his foot to close the door behind them. He then stripped the girl of her jacket. She could barely stand, let alone keep her eyes open.

"Almost there," Sam said as he guided the impaired girl through the house and into the living room.

Seeing the couch as a destination to lay down and recover for a moment, the girl stumbled her way towards the cushioned lounge. She no longer required Sam's guidance as she focused on her new-found destination.

"No, not there," Sam corrected as he placed a hand on the girl's shoulder and redirected her over towards the fireplace. "Wait right here. I have something special for you."

"You never can know," the girl said, slurring her words and swaying back and forth like a thin tree caught up in a storm's gust.

Know what?

"Aries and Scorpio knew, but Tyler and Aisha did not. How can you know what isn't known about the known current," she added as she looked out of the window nearest the fireplace. Her statement didn't make much sense and her gaze was endless into the darkness of the abyss. Induced by drugs, alcohol, or maybe just plain crazy, her mind was adrift and not within her head.

"You got it figured out," Sam agreed as he wrapped his fingers tightly around a fire iron that hung on the wall alongside the chimney. Slowly, he lifted the metal bar high above his head and silently crept up behind the girl. With all of his strength, he swung down on the back of her head. The girl's legs were fast to buckle out from under her as she collapsed to the floor.

Sam dropped the fire iron against the hardwood floor, which nicked a chunk out of the wood as it made a thud on contact. Then, kneeling down to the girl, Sam ran the tips of his fingers along the backside of her hands.

"Sorry, Miss, but I need these," he whispered calmly as he continued to caress her hands. He gently set them down against her chest, then retreated off to the basement to get something.

I hopped off the couch and walked over to the girl. She was far younger than most of the other girls that Sam would typically see.

At least this kill was quick and painless.

Sam re-entered the room wearing a mask and holding a power saw. I got out of his way and hopped back up onto the couch to watch him work.

Kneeling down to the girl, he gripped her left hand and activated the blade. It screamed like a tornado of broken glass that had gulped up a thousand damned souls from the fiercest pits of hell.

After detaching her left hand at the wrist, he moved on to the right one. Blood and tendons were quick to ooze their way out from her open forearms.

Sam stood up and walked away with his trophies: the girl's hands. He didn't get far before freezing in place when the girl made a noise.

Groaning, the girl tried to sit up. She was still *alive*. Her sedation flipped off like a switch when she noticed that not only were her hands gone, but her wrists were flowing blood like an uncontrollable hose that had been left turned on all throughout the night.

Sam looked at the girl. The expression on his face suggested that he was completely surprised by her resilience to death. He used one of her severed hands to press a finger of hers up against his mouth like he was deep in thought and perhaps even slightly impressed. Sam simply observed as the girl succumbed to a full-blown emotional breakdown. She screamed like I had never heard a girl scream before. Giving into a state of shock and blood loss, I don't think that she felt the physical pain of losing her hands. At the very least I wanted to believe that to be true. I have no doubt that her mind had shattered with thoughts of agony and terror at what had been done to her. That level of emotional torment exceeded any amount of physical pain that could have ever been inflicted onto her.

Coming to investigate the cause of stir, Rex posted up alongside Sam. Though holding himself back, Rex was ready to silence the girl at any given second. He patiently awaited Sam's discretion while watching the girl with both Sam and me, but unlike us, he was tense in posture. So tense that he looked as though he could snap at the drop of a pin.

Sam glanced down at Rex and then back to the girl, who was screaming and crying as she tried to understand what had happened to her. It felt like everything was unfolding in slow motion. Sam looked again to the pitbull who sat awaiting his command. With a nod forward that served as a green light gesture, Sam approved of Rex handling the situation.

Like a bullet being fired from a gun, the pitbull was off and across the room. He dove on top of the screaming girl and began ripping away at her face. Piece by piece, her skin was being shredded away like cheese being scraped against a grater. The girl fell back and struggled. It was hopeless. Rex continued sinking his teeth into the girl's face, snapping, shredding, pulling, and tearing at every fiber of her being. As she gave in to the overpowering dog and went limp, Sam turned and walked away.

In that moment, my theory of pain and tolerance was proven incorrect. I had thought that things could not have gotten any worse for the girl, but they had. They had gotten much worse. The only benefit to her existence now was that she was dead. Now her body was nothing more than an empty vessel of meat. Organs and flesh with no sense of consciousness. Lifelessly oblivious to the devour Rex unleashed upon it.

Sam locked himself down in the basement that night while Rex was up until the wee hours of the morning chewing on the corpse of the girl, whose name I did not know. I stayed on the couch and rested my head down on a pillow as I closed my eyes. The smell of blood in the room was strong; so strong that I could taste it in my mouth. I tried to go to sleep, but the sounds of both Sam hacking away in the basement and Rex gnawing at the carcass in the living room kept me awake. All night I listened to the two of them. At some point, I thought that I had heard, again, the faint moaning of a girl, alive and in torment, coming from downstairs. With wide eyes, I endured the discomforting horrors around me until the sun came up and the birds chirped a somewhat comforting song outside. Their presence was a symbol that unveiled a new day rising.

I jumped down from the couch. Rex was soundly asleep next to the dead girl. Her body was no longer recognizable even in the slightest accord. Most of her skin was gone and the meat that her flesh once held tightly on the inside was now sprawled out across the floor along with piles of torn entrails. Rex was covered in red.

I made way for the door in the kitchen that led outside. Soon, Sam would come upstairs and let me out, freeing me from this prison of death and decay; but he never came. Before long, the morning that had come had also gone away as the night forcefully declared it her time to reign supreme once more. Despite having to pee all day, I painfully held back the pains of my bladder and whined. Rex had arrived in the kitchen at some point, which forced me to leave. When he came back out to the living room, I scurried back into the kitchen to find that, at some point in the afternoon waiting for Sam, Rex had defecated all over the floor.

That is barbaric. This is our home. This is where we eat and this is where we sleep.

Now with the kitchen stinking of Rex's defile, I left and sat in the corner of the living room as to not disturb Rex. He was hungry from not being fed all day and decided to substitute the entrails of the dead girl on the floor as a meal. Listening to him chew and devour flesh that had already been shredded into heaps of liquefied mush was a tormenting experience to endure in and of itself.

I turned around and went back into the kitchen. I trudged through a pool of Rex's piss to get to the closed wooden door that led down into the basement.

Sam, come upstairs. I barked as I jumped at the cellar door and scratched against it. *Please, Sam! Please come upstairs and let me outside!* I continued scratching helplessly against the door. I wasn't even sure if he was down there, but I hadn't heard or seen him leave, so figured he must be down there still. *Please, Sam! Please!* I barked. The sound of my urine hitting the floor forced me to stop attacking the door. I simply couldn't hold it any longer and I was embarrassed. I found a spot in the bathroom, laid down, and began licking my paws to cleanse them of the pee in my fur. The moon was shining through the window, which meant it had been a full day now since we last saw Sam.

The next morning, I entered the kitchen to find that Rex had figured out how to get into the can where Sam stored our food. I wanted to be angry at Rex for digging in and devouring our reservoir, but I was starving and, my petty differences with him aside, I was grateful for him to have found us food.

I sat by the doorway and waited for Rex to finish eating. I knew the routine. I just hoped that there would be some left for me. As soon as he had his fill, he went over to the wall and laid himself down with a groan beside the fridge. The second he closed his eyes I bolted forward to the metal can of kibble. There were three stray bits in the end of the toppled over container. It would have felt less cruel if he had just finished what was left. I dipped my head into the can and ate the leftovers, then left the kitchen, feeling dizzy and weak with my tail in between my legs.

That's it for our food supply until Sam comes home. I hope he comes home soon.

It wasn't like Sam to be gone for so long and the way he had left was unsettling to say the least. He had just up and vanished in the middle of the night.

The blood and gore in the living room was beginning to rot and badly stink, so I went into the back room of the house. I hid behind a pile of dirty clothes and just tried to sleep for a while. My stomach ached and growled, demanding to be fed, which made trying to sleep all the more futile.

I am so hungry, I whined like a little puppy. *Please, Sam, just come home.*

After an afternoon of counting dust particles as they floated through the rays of sun that illuminated the room, I wandered out into the rest of the house. I passed the kitchen and casually glanced over to Rex. He was hunched over defecating onto the floor. He didn't seem to care that I had seen him this time but, in that moment, I realized that he was just as vulnerable, alone, and pathetic as I.

A few minutes later, I heard the steps of two men approaching the house from outdoors as their feet sloshed and sunk down into the mud that littered the driveway. The pattern and pace of a man is very different than that of a woman and, by the sounds that they made, I could tell their gender before ever even laying eyes on them.

Rex was asleep near the front door in the kitchen. So as not to wake him, I carefully made my way to a window in the living room to look out and see who it was that approached across the yard. As I predicted, it was two men: the two cops that had come to the house the day that Mia had died.

The two climbed the stairs of the porch. The skinner man turned to scan the yard behind them. In that moment, his unshaven face turned pale, which made him appear uneasy. It was almost as if perhaps he could sense that they were being watched. The larger man pounded on the door three times. He only really needed to knock once, for by the first blow on the door, Rex had awoken and sprung up against the glass.

Drooling at the mouth and snarling like the maniac that he was, he showed a true display of bloodlust; the utmost desire to shred and kill anyone and anything that dared to enter into our home.

The larger man pressed his face up against the window near the one I sat looking out of. Though his eyes were busy scanning the room for activity, he could not see me standing off to the side and in the shadows; it was something that I was truly grateful for as I began to succumb to a state of fear.

"Looks like our guy isn't home," he said, pulling his face away from the window.

"We knew that. His truck isn't here. Come on, let's get out of here and wait on the warrant. Leon said it should be ready to go by four," suggested the slimmer man, Kyle.

It was extremely difficult trying to make out their conversation with Rex carrying on and acting a fool in the kitchen, but I focused my attention on the reverberations of their voices and homed in on their pitches of sound.

"No wait," ordered the larger man as he turned back to face the door, "You see that?"

"See what?"

The larger man withdrew what looked to be a small crowbar from within his trench coat, then he lodged it gently in between the front door and its frame.

"Don't do this, Steve, you will get our entire fucking case thrown out," the skinnier detective warned.

"Tired of waiting around for this cocksucker. For all we know, he skipped town a few days ago when we last had eyes on him."

"Just wait a few more hours for the warrant, Steve."

"A warrant? The door is cracked open and that beast is lunging straight at my partner," he added as the door gave way to him having jimmied it ajar. The door gave off a creak as it slowly drifted open.

Like clockwork, Rex didn't waste the slightest of seconds

to jump through the air and attack the two men. Anticipating the assault, the larger man, Steve, withdrew a pistol from his jacket and fired. Each squeeze of the trigger sounded as though lightning were being cast into the house. I was frozen in place, watching in horror as Rex dropped to the ground and bled out on the porch. He was well past dead by the fourth or fifth shot, but that did not stop the man from emptying his magazine, fifteen rounds total into my friend.

Scared to my wits' end, I pissed all over the floor.

As the larger man turned to the skinnier one, he smiled and uttered the words, "Wasted that bitch."

They were now entering the house and, at last, my brain forced my legs to move. As I bolted for the back room and hid in a dark corner, I prayed that they would not find and 'waste' me like they had done Rex. I buried myself amongst a pile of dirty clothes, but the disguise did me little good as I began to tremble uncontrollably. I could hear their footsteps clicking on the hardwood floor as they slowly walked through the house. I cried out minor yelps and squeals as my legs shook in a radical fashion beneath me.

They are going to find me. They are going to kill me!

The door to the laundry room in which I hid was opened, but not fully. One of the men placed a hand on the wooden door and gently gave it a push. It creaked loudly as it slowly drifted open. Again I was peeing all over myself and the floor as I trembled in place amongst the pile of dirty clothes.

Standing in the doorway was the larger cop. His eyes were locked onto mine. With his weapon pointed at me, he had a facial expression that suggested he needed no reason to end my life like he had done to Rex. I knew then that I was going to die. His stance was firm and his legs were planted with a gap in between them. I figured I could squeeze between his legs and escape, so drastically, I made my break. I barely managed to move a paw before the man fired his gun at me. Four loud pops that made my ears ring also sent me to the floor squealing and crying.

I heard the skinnier guy begin to shout as he pushed his way into the room and dropped down to the floor. He pressed his hand up against the holes in my body that were quickly bleeding me dry. I began to feel lightheaded and lost my strength to continue squealing any longer as everything went white and I died on the floor, choking in a pool of my own blood.

ACT II

Afterlife

Chapter 7

High Beams

I came to, feeling as though reality were nothing more than a dream. Everything felt hazy and blurry.

Is this the afterlife?

I could hear voices conversing nearby. I forced my eyes open to see the fuzzy silhouette of a man. As my vision centered its focus, I noticed that I was actually in a brightly lit room with two men. One of the men was practically on top of me. He was wearing a white lab coat over top his buttoned up, collared shirt and tie. A facemask disguised his mouth and chin. I could see his eyes; they were big, soft, and blue.

Am I not dead?

The man plucked his rubber gloves off and tossed them away into a waste bin. Then, by a set of white straps behind his bald head, he removed the blue mask that covered his face. His skin was old and loose with pockets of wrinkles and white stray hairs. I could sense that his soul was just as gentle as his physique. Maybe that was something that came with age.

"So what really happened with that nut job?" the doctor questioned.

The man he was talking to looked familiar. I soon realized that it was one of the cops that had come into the house; it was the skinnier one with the prickly, unshaven face.

"I don't know, I guess he caught wind that we were looking into him and skipped town. Steve was reckless with our investigation and I think the guy picked up on us eavesdropping on him. After we discovered the basement, the case got handed over to the feds. What a monster. That basement. I have never seen anything like it in my ten years on the streets."

"News said that he had cut up girls and pieced them back together with one another. Is there any truth in that?"

"Yeah. I don't know how it got leaked to the media, but yeah. Only I'm telling you, Dad, it was a million times worse than anything you could ever imagine. He didn't just cut up and disassemble limbs, he used precision to piece together a master vision that could be sewn, stapled, and nailed into place. I couldn't bear to look at the monstrosity he created for very long. Our forensics guy, Neville, said he thought the guy was even having sex with the thing."

"Were the girls alive when he cut them up?"

"From what I heard, yeah."

"Jesus ... that's insane," the old doctor said with his eyes bulged.

"Sure is... The strange thing about guys like this, though, is that generally, they have a deep connection with their work. So much so that skipping town and leaving it behind is not really ever an option. Typically, when profiles like this abandon their masterpiece, it is because they are finished with it and want someone to find it, but it doesn't mean they are finished doing what it is that they do. They are just ready for the next creation."

The old man slowly nodded his head and furrowed his brows as he rolled his lips in towards his mouth.

"Steve and I were so close to grabbing this fuck, and he slipped right through our fingers," the cop added. "I guess none of that matters now, though. The case is out of my hands..."

After a moment of silence passed, the older man changed the topic of their conversation. "So what are you going to do with him now?" The gesture he made with his head and hand suggested he was speaking about me.

"Well, I was thinking about keeping him. Mary could use a friend around the house about now."

"That's not a bad idea. What are you going to tell her about where he came from?"

"Christ, I don't know. That he is a rescue, I guess. It's technically true, but the details need to stay between us. God knows she doesn't need more worry in her life."

My full body paralysis seemed to be subsiding as I slowly regained control of my limbs. I moved my feet back and forth as if I were walking and trying to escape, though really I was laying on my side and simply flailing like a fool. It was a relief to know that my feet worked.

"Well, look who is awake," the doctor said as he leaned in with a smile.

He gently pulled the skin below my eyelids down and then briefly shined a bright flashlight into each of them, one at a time.

My side began to throb and I couldn't help but whine as I struggled, yet failed, to get up.

"Woah there, champ," the doctor eased. "Looks like those anesthetics are wearing off. I will get you some painkillers."

He pulled a lanyard with a set of keys fixed to the end from his pocket and walked over to a locked cabinet. I wanted to turn my head to see what he was doing inside of the cupboard, but lifting my head was not something I could do easily at the moment.

The cop came a little closer to me and put his hand on my neck. He was running his fingers through my fur, but I couldn't feel it. "When do you think I can take him home?" he asked.

Yes, please take me home. I do not want to be on this table any longer. I want to see Sam. Please just take me home.

"Well, no reason you can't take him home today. Just have to make sure he doesn't pick at those stitches when he gets his energy back. You are probably going to want to put a cone on him so he doesn't."

"Yeah, I will keep a close eye on him."

Leaving the doctor's office and driving home seemed a blur. Before long, I awoke to find myself sitting in the middle of a foreign living room. It was hard to recollect the time in between laying on the table in the doctor's office and arriving where I now found myself. The living room that I was in belonged to a foreign house. The walls were a funky sort of color that I had never seen before. Somewhere between blue and white, the paint looked fresh as if it was newly applied sometime earlier in the year.

Sitting on the floor in front of me was a woman. She was tall and very thin. Her skin was pale and her eyes sunken in, which led me to assume that perhaps she was sick. Nevertheless, she was pretty. She was wearing brown pants and a low cut tee shirt. She had shoulder length brown hair that was choppy in its styling and her eyes were matched with the same shade of brown as her hair. Her eyes were also dilated and locked into a stare with mine. I would have felt uncomfortable with her awkward gaze if her face hadn't been radiating with the excitement that she seemed to exert from head to toe. For what she was so pleased about, I did not exactly know.

"He is awake," she squealed with joy. Her voice was soft and appealing.

"Just be gentle, OK? We don't want to overwhelm him," The officer from before, Kyle, said as he entered the room with a hot cup of coffee in hand. He was dressed casually in cargo shorts and a tee shirt.

The girl gave him a gentle nod, then turned back to face me. "Hi, Linus, I am Mary and this is Kyle," she informed me with an outstretched palm.

I felt weak and out of it, but her aroma was that of a sweet sort of flower that I had never smelled before. I leaned forward to sniff her hand and ponder the scent. Using her other hand, she slowly reached in and began patting me on the head. It was the ole bait and switch. Lure me in via tapping into my curiosity, then spring the trap onto me as if you are allowed to do as such. I pulled back just far enough to be out of her reach.

Don't touch me! I don't know you, Lady! Where am I?

"It's okay," she eased.

No! It's not okay! I need to get out of here and go home! Sam might be back and waiting for me. He is going to want to know where I am!

"Just give him a little space, Mary," Kyle said. "He has to get used to his new home."

New home? This is not my home! I have a home!

"Okay," Mary agreed with a frown.

"I am going to run out and grab dog food. Do we need anything else?" Kyle asked as he walked out to the kitchen with his coffee cup.

"Cheshire needs food, too," Mary answered as she stood up from the floor and followed him out of the room.

Who is Cheshire?

I glanced around the room and froze when I spotted a cat gawking my way. It was a fluffy little ball of long, black fur that really served to creep me out.

The hell are you lookin' at, Man?

With its stone-cold dilated pupils, the cat watched me as I approached.

Hey you!

The cat was frozen in place. Maybe it thought not moving would work as a means of defense, camouflaging it before my very eyes.

You do know that I can see you, right?

I leaned in and smelled him. Turns out he was actually she. Cheshire oozed feminine pheromones that placed emphasis on her current level of fear.

Maybe I should back off.

Just as soon as I began to pull back, Cheshire puffed up her fur like a balloon. Her face shifted into the form of some evil demonic monster and she hissed as she swiped her claws across my face. It all happened so fast. I squealed out in fright as I limped out of the living room and towards the front door.

"Linus, what's wrong?" Mary said as she came over to me.

With blood in my eyes, I realized just how badly Cheshire had dug into me. The fresh cuts on my face began to sting and burn.

Please, I just want to go back home. Let me outside so that I can go home.

"Awe, you're bleeding," Mary groaned. "Wait right here," she instructed as she went back into the kitchen. I leaned over to see her reach for a washcloth and dampen it under warm water. She then came back to me and knelt down to my level as she gently placed a hand on my face. I flinched and she said, "Sit still and I will clean you up." The cuts stung as she cleaned them with her wet cloth. "You should stay away from Cheshire. She is a grumpy old cat who has never lived with a dog before."

You could have warned me about that before leaving me alone in a room with her.

When Mary was done, she took the bloody cloth into another room with a large and bright window. I followed her in to watch her toss the rag into a laundry basket, then she stood by the window and looked out into a garden that was hidden away in the back yard. Large trees and shrubs that concealed the garden from the sky were now turning yellow and brown with the change of seasons. Autumn was settling in.

I need to get out of here. Please, I just need to go home, I pleaded behind her with a slight whine.

She turned to face me, looking sad, then sat down on the floor with me. Her eyes were watery and I had to wonder if it was because of something I had done. When dogs cry, it isn't the tearful sort of sorrow that a human exerts, so typically humans never really understand when a dog is sad. Mary leaned in and gave me a hug. I don't know if it was to comfort me or comfort herself but, for a moment, it seemed to do both.

After a few minutes of the warm embrace, Mary said "I am going to take a shower."

She stood up and left the room. I followed. She then went into the bathroom and closed the door, which left me alone in the strange house with the demon cat who lurked in the shadows. Despite feeling the need to escape, my wounds with the stitches ached, so I decided it best to lay down and rest for a while. As I closed my eyes, I heard something jump up onto a shelf that was in the same room as I. While keeping my head flat on the ground, I opened and lifted my eyes to see that the cat was spying on me. She was on a ledge high above trying to squeeze her way behind a large glass picture frame. I stood up and watched her acrobat her way onto another platform that had little glass vases on it. This platform was loose and it wobbled under the weight of her feet.

Hey, you better get down before that breaks and you fall, I barked while standing up to get a better look.

My howl startled the cat. She flipped through the air to turn around and run away. In her careless retreat, the platform she was on loosened and buckled. I watched as it free-fell and crashed into the shelf directly below it. All of the contents of both platforms dropped to the floor and shattered into a million little pieces right in front of me. Cheshire bolted from the room and out of sight, leaving me to the mess.

Wearing nothing but a towel, Mary scurried out of the bathroom with her hair soaking wet. "Linus, what have you done?" she cried in seeing the shattered bits of glass below my feet.

It wasn't me. It was the cat.

Mary dropped to the floor and picked up one of the broken bits. "This was my mother's," she explained. Then, with a sob, she reached for the large picture, whose frame was all but gone. In the picture was herself smiling in a large white gown. An older woman was standing closely to her right and Kyle was standing to the left with an older man and woman to his side. With tears in her eyes, Mary ran her fingers across the picture. The glass frame had torn and distorted the image when it had fallen and shattered. With bits of broken glass digging into her soft fingers, Mary pulled the picture inwards and began to cry as blood trickled down her hands and onto the floor. She stood up and walked into the kitchen with the photo. I followed and stood by the door.

Just let me outside and I will go away.

After plucking the broken glass from her fingers and rinsing the blood from her hands, she wrapped her fingers with little bandages and turned to face me. "Do you have to go outside?" she asked with a sniffle as she regained control of her emotions.

Yes. Yes, I do.

Mary threw a robe on over her towel and fastened it tightly closed. She then walked over and opened the door. I stepped through the door and exited the house. Once outside, I looked up to the sky, which was skewn with darkened clouds. I inhaled the fresh air that washed over me. The rise of my chest in taking a deep breath hurt the wounds on my sides, but I tried best to press the thought of pain from my mind. I had to focus on getting home. The air was filled with moisture, which suggested that rain was inevitably inbound. Leaves were falling down from the trees at an accelerated rhythm as the wind picked up. The ones that already littered ground crunched as I walked over them. I advanced to the edge of the yard, where the grass met the pavement of the street. Houses ran down the block; none of which looked familiar in the slightest.

"Linus, stay in the yard," Mary cautioned as she stepped down from the porch and into the grass. "Oh no, maybe I should have placed you on a leash."

I turned back to look at her only for a brief moment. I had made up my mind long before ever stepping outside and, without another moment's hesitation, I bolted off down the street.

"Linus!" Mary pleaded as she ran across the yard barefoot.

Before she could make it to the sidewalk, I had turned the corner and vanished out of sight. Though I wasn't particularly sure as to which way was home, I somehow knew where it was I was heading.

Raindrops began to thump down onto the ground and, before long, my coat was wet and heavy as I trudged on in what was shaping up to be an evening thunderstorm. At some point I had to stop and seek shelter underneath a large pine tree as crackles of lightning lit up the murky welkin.

I have no idea where I am, I admitted to myself. I looked to the sky to see a moon faintly peak its way out from behind the clouds that pelted the ground with rain at a now violent rate. I moved out from the shelter that the tree provided and pressed on across a large field, whose tall grass was losing a battle against the winds of the storm to stand up straight. Lightning struck over the hills of the horizon. I knew that I wouldn't have long to get out of this field and to safety before the destructive bolts came my way. Though hindered by my wounds, I did my best to run across the field and make it onto another street. I don't remember how exactly I had done it, but after twenty minutes of trudging through the assault of a rainstorm, I somehow reached home. Things were different. There was yellow caution tape wrapped around the house, its windows, and its doors. *This is the house, though. I am sure of that much,* I reminded myself as I approached the home.

Two cops were sitting in a car across the street. I assumed they were standing guard, so if I wanted to enter and find Sam, I would have to be sneaky as to not get caught. Focusing on them not seeing me, I failed to realize that someone had gotten out of a car that was parked directly behind me.

"I figured I would find you here," Kyle said as he approached me from behind. "A dog's sense of direction is truly incredible."

His appearance startled me and I flinched.

"It's okay," he said as he hunched down in the rain and placed a hand on my wet, soggy head.

No longer caring if the two cops in their vehicle saw me, I set off across the street for home.

"Linus, wait. Stay," Kyle ordered.

You are not the alpha male in my pack. Sam is. Hell, you are not even a part of our pack.

As Kyle sprinted after me, I picked up my own pace to keep a gap between us. My sides ached and disagreed with my running, but I did not care. The two officers exited their car as they spotted me, and Kyle yelled something to them, which forced them to back down.

Through the yard and up the steps I squeezed myself past the thick collection of caution tape and made it into my house. Everything was just as it was last I was there. I could sense that Sam had not been back since his departure.

Kyle tore down the tape to the front door and entered in behind me. Our eyes met as he said, "He is not here, Linus."

I had to be sure. Dropping my nose to the floor, I saw the dry pool of blood left on the ground from Rex. He was such a monster, but he didn't deserve to die like he had.

I sniffed around and ran off to the living room. Human scents confirmed that men and women had been recently inside the house, but there was no trace of Sam. A large red stain was left on the floor from where the remains of Sam's last girlfriend once were. The stain was outlined in white chalk. With still no scent of Sam, I dashed through the house and began to whine.

With folded arms, Kyle stood watching me as I made my way into the room that I had hidden within the day his partner had attacked me. Dried out blotches of my own blood were stained up against the wall and a pool of evaporated urine was also close by, but still I picked up no scent of Sam having been there.

I ran back into the kitchen and over to the basement door, which had a fresh set of locks on it. Jumping up against the door, I felt the stitches in my side pull at my skin. It was painful, but still I pressed on in trying to open the door. It was my only real hope as to where Sam was, and I had to find him. In the back of my mind, I knew he wasn't down there, but I was desperate for answers. Barking and howling, I rammed my body against the door, but it would not give.

Kyle unfolded his arms and walked over to me. He hunched down to my level and looked directly into my face while gently scratching my soaking wet neck.

Where has he gone?... Why did he leave me? I whined and cried out loud in heartache. I was always such a weak pup, and maybe that is why Sam had left me in this house to die. *He was my best friend and I loved him.*

Kyle eased my cry with a gentle pat. It was as if he understood me and felt sorry. I wasn't looking for pity, but it felt good to have someone act as though they cared.

We left the house and Kyle escorted me to his car. On the ride back to his place, he wrapped me in a towel and dried off my wet coat. Once we arrived back to Kyle's house, Mary welcomed us inside by opening the door with a warm smile on her face.

I didn't fight Kyle in returning to his domain. He wasn't family, Mary wasn't family, and, least of all, Cheshire wasn't family, but where else could've I gone? At least Kyle offered me warm shelter, company, and food; all things that Sam no longer provided.

"Where did you find him?" Mary questioned.

"A few blocks down the street," Kyle lied.

"Well, I am glad you are back, Linus," Mary said with a wide smile that stretched from cheek to cheek.

Really?

Kyle looked down to me with a smirk of his own. As if reading my mind, he nodded and patted me on the head.

So, Mary is allowed to stay in the house when you are gone? Sam's girlfriends never had free reign of the house. They could only hang out in the house briefly before he moved them down into the basement.

I slowly entered the house, which was warm and smelled of some sweet sort of pastry. Four small pumpkins were laid out on the table and Mary slowly shuffled over to them.

"Are we still doing that?" Kyle asked as he peeled off his wet coat and tossed it over a hook in the wall beside the door.

"Yeah, well, unless you don't want to," Mary said hesitantly.

Kyle looked over a handful of tools that Mary had laid out in our absence. "No, I do," he said with a smile.

"There is a sub on the counter if you want to eat before we start," Mary said as she began taking the pumpkins individually into the living room where she set them down on the hardwood floor.

Kyle grabbed the sandwich and a pumpkin, then followed her into the living room. I slowly slinked my way in and noticed that the broken bits of glass, along with the fallen shelves, were cleaned up and gone. Cheshire was sitting on the couch, watching me as I entered into the living room.

Hey, Cheshire. I will keep my distance.

All four pumpkins were now on the floor. Mary, with trembling joints, took a seat on the ground.

"So, we are carving all four?" Kyle inquired.

"Yeah. One for me, one for you, one for Cheshire, and one for Linus," Mary said with glee.

"Okay," Kyle obliged with a smile as he took a seat beside her and finished his sandwich. "You like turkey, Linus?"

Yes!

I bolted to his side and wagged my tail. Just as soon as Kyle had handed me a sliver of the delicate white meat, I had inhaled it and slobbered all over his fingers. He laughed and Mary rolled her eyes whilst shaking her head with a smirk.

Picking up his tools, Kyle began cutting into the tops of the four large, orange vegetables. He then went on to separate their heads from their bodies. After all four had their crowns removed, Kyle reached his hand inside of one and pulled out a stringy mess of the squash's guts.

"Here, place the insides in this bucket," Mary said, sliding a pail in between herself and Kyle. "I will separate the seeds and bake them with some paprika later."

"How about I place the insides on *your* bucket," Kyle said with a chuckle as he hovered a handful of the goo over Mary's head.

"Don't do it," Mary warned. Though she was trying to be serious, she was not the least bit intimidating in her stance.

With a smirk on his face, Kyle dropped the bits of pumpkin innards onto the top of her head. He didn't seem to care in the slightest how irate Mary had become. She reached into the container beside her and flung a handful of the stringy mess at Kyle's face. This triggered an all-out war between the two of them as they laughed and flung the mess back and forth at each other. Cheshire bolted out of the room and up the stairs to safety. Getting dirty seemed to not be her sort of thing.

Kyle slapped a handful of the orange guts onto my head and Mary burst into laughter. It felt gooey and wet. I pulled my head back and some of the strands slipped down the side of my face, which forced Kyle to now join in on laughing at me. A chunk fell to the floor and I gave it a sniff. It was something I had never smelled before. I licked it and immediately scrunched up my face. The taste was odd, but I kind of liked it.

"Does Linus like pumpkin?" Mary said with a giggle.

Yeah, I guess I do.

On the floor and covered in the pumpkin mess, the three of us shared in a moment of happiness and laughter.

Maybe it was for the better that Sam left the way that he had. Mary and Kyle seemed happy together and, though I was an outsider, they seemed welcoming of my presence.

***

After a night of sleeping by the fireplace of my new home, I awoke to find Kyle and Mary in the kitchen. It was late into the morning. I guess, given the wounds on my side, my body had forced me to sleep in to recover a bit. Kyle poured a glass of orange juice and placed it in front of Mary. He then poured himself one and began to quickly drink it.

"Tomorrow, I am going sit down with the chief and address my concerns," he said after finishing his glass and setting it down.

"What do you think he will do?"

"I don't know. I mean, he knows this is going on, he has to; he isn't stupid. So either he does something about it, or he reassigns me to traffic duty for a few months until it all blows over. Everybody hates traffic duty. It is considered the bottom of the barrel, but I honestly don't think that I would mind. Working alone and being away from those guys for a while would be pretty great."

"That doesn't do anything to address or fix the problem, though," Mary pointed out.

Kyle raised his eyebrows and sighed. "A lot easier to act

deaf, dumb, and blind towards a problem than fix it."

"All he has to do is fire the bad eggs in the department," Mary stated.

"Yeah, but all these guys stick together. When the media catches wind that there is a cleansing within the department of the wicked and corrupt, they will blow the story into a resolution fit for crucifixion. People don't care about the shit that happens around them unless it personally and directly affects themselves or the media tells them that they should care."

Mary looked down to her full glass of orange juice like a child who had lost her way. She then glanced back up to Kyle. "So, what are you going to do today?"

Kyle rinsed out his glass out, then refilled it with water. "I am going to run out and get paint; finish up that porch," he paused to throw the glass of water down his throat. "Wanna come?"

I perked my ears up to clarify that he was talking to Mary and not me.

"No, I'm okay," she said with a sigh.

"Come on, you have got to get out once in a while, Mary," he pleaded, placing a hand onto her shoulder.

"I know. I will," she said with a faint, forced smile. "I am just really tired and think I am going to take a nap."

Without saying anything, Kyle pressed his lips inward on top of one another and nodded. "What about you?" he asked, looking in my direction. "Want to go for a ride?"

For a brief moment, I completely lost it. I dipped my head low and jumped up and down. My side shrieked out in pain from my still healing wounds, but my tail flew back and forth like the wings of a hummingbird. For a second, I thought that I may very well take flight off the ground.

Mary laughed.

"I knew *you* would," Kyle said with a laugh. "Okay, I will see you in a bit," he added as he planted a kiss on Mary's cheek.

Just as soon as Kyle laced up his shoes and threw on a jacket, both he and I were out the door. I glanced back to see Mary staring down at the glass of orange juice in front of her that had gone untouched. A part of me felt as though I should go back inside and keep her company, but when Kyle lifted the garage door, I lost my train of thought to curiosity. In the garage sat a red BMW convertible. I had wondered what it was he may keep in the garage and I was relieved to see it was a car and not the dead bodies of young women.

I love cars. Love chasing them, love watching them, and love riding in them.

I had never seen one quite like this before and was left to assume that this model was old and long since outdated. The soft top was a little worn-out looking, but there was not a scratch on the paint of the car itself.

Kyle opened the door to the car and he didn't have to twist my paw to get me to jump in. In fact, I was so excited that I leaped into the car almost as soon as he had opened the door. He climbed in behind me and started it up. The low rumble of the engine raised the hairs on the back of my neck.

After clicking in a lever on the roof, Kyle gave it a quick twist, then pushed up on it. I could hear the faint hum of a small motor as the top shell of the car lowered down and out of sight. We were fully exposed on all sides to the world around us.

Woah, this is awesome!

Kyle reached over and fastened a seatbelt across my chest. I had never been required to wear one when riding with Sam, but with Kyle's car being so open to the outside, I was okay with the extra sense of security.

"Ready?" Kyle asked with a smile.

Sure am.

We pulled out onto the road and set off on our adventure. The morning air was crisp and cool. The warmth that I felt on the inside for the joys of our travel burned hot enough to compensate for any sort of cold front that may cross our path.

Kyle scratched my neck with one hand and steered the car with another as we worked our way through the city. I flung my tongue out from the side of my face and smiled. I could see it all, life through a looking glass. And it was a marvelous sort of looking glass, indeed.

We turned down a side road, which led us out from the city's center. We then climbed up over a hill that was covered with trees that were painted in the colors of autumn. The hill lowered and crashed into another. We climbed and repeated our fall as the setting continued its shift to the landscapes of the countryside. A misty sort of fog lingered on these roads. It raised up from the pavement and skewed our vision of the hills in the distance. It was eerie to say the least. Like lost souls of the damned wandering on the racetracks of eternity with no place to go.

Hey, look, a deer.

Clearly, I saw the doe long before Kyle had, as we accelerated in the car towards the spot where the deer was stuck frozen, scared on the side of the road. The moment the beams of the car's headlights lit up the deer's face, Kyle too saw the doe. He tried to swerve to miss it and would have if the hooved creature hadn't panicked at the last second. Diving directly in front of us, the doe slammed into the front of the car and flew up over top of us. I pitched forward on the impact and the seatbelt that was strewn across my chest gripped me back into my seat. The tires of the car screeched and we began spinning out of control until we flew over a ditch and into a field, ultimately landing to a stop.

"*Fuck!*" Kyle screamed, breathing heavily. He looked behind us and then over to me. "You alright?"

I am okay.

"You stay here," Kyle ordered while unbuckling his seatbelt and jumping out of the car.

Just as he disappeared into the darkness, I squeezed down and out of the seat belt. Feeling a sharp sting, I looked down to see that the harness that had held me in place was smeared red with blood. I was bleeding, but in the adrenaline rush from getting in an accident, I didn't even notice that my stitches had torn open against the seat belt. I limped over to the door Kyle had left open when he had exited the car. I then hopped down into the grass. Kyle had walked back to the road and found the deer, who was still alive, lying on the ground.

"I told you to stay in the car," Kyle said when he saw me limp up behind him. "Sit. Stay," he urged, and this time, I listened.

The deer on the ground had its front legs snapped on impact. They were bent completely backwards with bits of bone sticking out from the lesions. One of its eyes were hanging down and out from the socket and the doe was struggling to breathe. Its chest was torn open and bits of meat were hanging out like an opened container of spaghetti sauce that had spilled across the floor. As Kyle got closer, the doe tried to get up. It was futile. The deer quickly realized it was going nowhere and laid itself back down while still struggling to maintain its sense of existence.

"Shit," Kyle said softly under his breath. From under his jacket, he withdrew his revolver and pointed it at the deer's head. The deer didn't close its one good eye, rather, it looked directly into Kyle's face until the gun went off and the blast ended its life. The crack of the weapon firing echoed for miles in every direction. I didn't flinch. I stood firm in watching Kyle kill the doe. It was the right thing to do. Perhaps the deer could have fought to live another hour or two, but to maintain your animation in that kind of agony for hours on end was something I knew that I could never do.

Kyle reached down and grabbed the deer by its hind legs and dragged it from the road so that no car coming down this dangerous path would accidentally hit it like we had. After the deer was off and into the bushes, Kyle returned to me with blood on his hands.

"Come on, let's get out of here," he said softly.

When we got back to the car, I jumped up and got into my seat, and Kyle climbed in after. He noticed the blood in my seat that belonged to neither himself nor the deer. He then looked at me with a face of horror. "Are you bleeding?"

Yeah. It's okay, though.

The pain I felt was somewhat subdued by how quickly my heart was still racing.

Kyle reached over and felt my side, where my wounds were. He withdrew his hand, which was wet and sticky with my blood. "Christ," he muttered. He then started up the car and pulled back onto the road.

As we drove away, I saw a young fawn climb out from the bushes where it had hidden away during the accident. It was walking over to the dead doe in the field behind us.

Chapter 8

All Black Everything

Kyle rushed me over to the vet, his father, who had patched me up a few days prior.

Here I am, back on this table in the overly bright room that smells all too much like latex.

Kyle's father picked up a syringe and filled it with a clear liquid from a glass vial. He squirted a few drops into the air and then brought the needle over towards me.

"Go ahead and grab hold of him."

Kyle reached over top of me and held me firmly in place, while redirecting my head away so that I could not see what was going on.

"So, how are you liking your new home, Mister?" Kyle's father asked as he pricked me with the needle.

I... I like it there. I would really like to see what is going on.

I squirmed a bit to try and look at what was happening, but Kyle held me in place as my brain began to feel fuzzy. It was as if my head was filled to the brim with clouds that were gently spilling out and running down the side of my face. I also felt light, so light that I was going to float up and away from the table that I was on top of and hit my head on the roof of the room.

Kyle loosened his grip on me as I laid myself back and embraced the intoxication. It was hard to keep hold of any train of thought for too long. While the two of them spoke for a few minutes, it took me a moment to break into a sense of listening.

"Well, what does Mary think?" Kyle's dad asked as he worked on my open wound.

"I don't know, I mean, I spoke to her this morning and she was supportive, as usual. In her eyes, I can do no wrong with handling the situation, which is a relief, but I need legit advice here, Dad."

"Well, that's really a tough situation, Son."

"People are mad that we let Sam get away, and they should be. But no one is mad about the ongoing corruption in the department. It's like the chief is letting the media crucify us over Sam Martin so that it distracts the public away from what we are *really* doing wrong.

"And that is?"

"Psh, don't even get me started. Extortion, racketeering, and police brutality are just a handful of infections that plague my department. I mean, if the oath to protect and serve was ever taken, it was done so with one's own self-interest at heart."

Hey, Kyle, am I drooling on myself?

"Last year, when we were on the Larsky case," Kyle continued as he rubbed my face, "Steven took shortcuts at every turn to get probable cause and while, yeah, Larsky prolly did do it... I still stay awake at night wondering; you know... what if he hadn't? What if the guy had his entire life torn apart by a handful of cops on a power trip because he was simply at the wrong place at the wrong time? Every day the amount of pressure on my shoulders is multiplied with the things that I hear and the things that I see well before heading out and doing my job. I mean, the first portion of my day typically consists of listening to my colleagues joke around about that kid they killed last year. Just because the charges were dropped doesn't mean it is in good taste to be making jokes about it. That kid was somebody's son and they have made a habit out of cracking jokes about the boy on a daily basis."

"Well, you are a man, and a good one at that. You will do what you will do and I think that you made up your mind as to what *that* was well before coming to me today."

"Yeah," Kyle said with a sigh, turning his gaze down towards me. "No one wants to work with a whistleblower. I can kiss my career goodbye, and while I'm willing to risk that in order to do what is right, I know I can't afford to lose our health-care plan; not with Mary in her current condition."

"You know, your mother and I will help with what we can towards those hospital bills, Kyle," Kyle's dad comforted as he tore off his gloves and spritzed the area he was working on with water.

"I could never ask that of you guys. God knows you two need what you have anyway, given mom's health. These hospitals are fuckin' cash labs. I mean shit, Dad, you should see the size of the bills we have now, and that is *with* health-care. Besides, it won't just be the health plan that I will lose. Every cop in New York will know my name. They will hate me, hunt me down, and hang me out to dry if they catch me... I should have just stayed with the family business. When I went off to the academy, why didn't you convince me to go off to a vet school like Katie and Cole?

"Me and your mother did our best to support you kids in whatever decision you guys made. Would have loved to see you join in on the family biz, but you wanted to be a cop, *and you made it, Kyle.* Not only are you one, but you're a damn fine one at that. With so much bullshit going on in the world today, communities need people like you, Son."

"The sickness is too great, Dad. The infection runs deep; too deep for a culling or a cure. I'm no solution; no syringe filled with some magical antidote. I'm merely an idea..."

"And sometimes that's all people need, Son," Kyle's father concluded. He joined his son in looking down at me. "Well, how you feeling, Champ?" he asked me as he gently rubbed my nose with his large, wrinkled hands.

This place is just so great. At first I didn't like being here, but every time I am, you inject me with the fuzz juice that makes everything feel fluffy and happy. You two are just great, you know that?

Kyle's father reached for a towel and wiped away a bunch of drool from my mouth that I was not even aware was there.

Sorry about that.

"You met Cheshire, I see," Kyle's father pointed out as he touched the scratches on my face.

Yeah, she doesn't like me very much.

"Mean old cat. Never did like cats all too much," Kyle admitted.

"I like cats, but your mother being allergic to both cats and dogs meant we could never have any," Kyle's father stated. He cleaned the cuts on my face with a cold, clear liquid and a cotton ball.

"Well, it's a good thing you get your fix at work then, eh Dad?" Kyle said with a smile. "You remember that time someone brought in a stray dog and you patched him up and brought him home? Mom tried to play it cool because she knew that you felt bad for the damn thing and just wanted to help it," Kyle added with a laugh.

"Yeah, God bless that woman. She was miserable for weeks while I treated that dog at home. Poor little guy didn't survive but about three weeks until that infection took hold of him," Kyle's dad said with a frown as he discarded the bloody cotton balls into the trash. "This guy, however," he said, rubbing my face with a smile, "is good to go once again. Can you stand up for me?"

In an attempt to impress him, I got up to my feet as quickly as possible. I didn't make it far in rising as I immediately lost control of my balance and fell back down. I would have rolled right off of the table if Kyle and his father hadn't caught me in the air.

"Looks like I will have to carry you out to the car," Kyle said as he pulled me up into his arms with what looked like ease.

Being carried always was embarrassing, but neither Kyle nor his father seemed to judge as we made it outside and the two placed me into the front seat.

"Well, that doesn't look too bad," Kyle's father said as he hunched down to inspect the front of the car where we had smashed into the deer.

"Yeah, it should just be a little buffer and repaint job. These old BMW's are built like tanks."

"Well, there is a reason the Germans had them making jet engines for the Luftwaffe in World War II,"

The luf-what?

"I will see you later, Dad," Kyle said as he hopped into the car. "Thanks again."

I slept on the car ride back. Once home and awake I tried to fight off my conscience, which beckoned me to again succumb to a state of slumber. As I sat by the warmth of the fireplace, I began to nod back off to sleep while Kyle and Mary talked on the couch and Cheshire lingered in the shadows of the house.

I awoke in the morning refreshed and approached Mary, who was on the couch staring aimlessly out the window. I broke her glare as I placed my head down next to her hand.

"Good morning, Handsome," she said with a smile as she

patted me gently on my face." How are you feeling?"

I feel great, but I am also really hungry.

Kyle entered the room with a plate of food that smelled of maple and butter in one hand and a glass of orange juice in the other. He handed the warm plate to Mary with a smile that forced her to droop her eyes and fire back a smile of gratification.

"Do you remember when we got married and I said that as long as you make me blueberry pancakes, I will love you unconditionally and forever?"

Kyle smirked, "It is by no mistake that I have crafted such a masterful collection of little blueberry stuffed breakfast cakes for you on this morning."

He reached in with his head and placed a gentle kiss onto the side of her cheek. She forced a delicate smile as she accepted his sign of reverence from lips reserved only for her. She softened her eyes as he pulled away to take leave for the day.

"I might be home late depending on how things go with the chief today," he declared as he snagged up one of the blueberries from her plate and popped it into his mouth before slinging his jacket up over his shoulder.

"I know," she said with comfort and understanding in her tone.

I was never one for fruits, but even I had to admit, those ripe little things looked delicious scattered across the plate of warm food.

"See you later, Buddy," Kyle added, glancing at me before taking his leave.

Peace out, Man.

"I love you," she said softly as he took leave for the door.

Stopping to turn and face her, he replied, "I love you, too."

She waited for Kyle to leave, then she placed the hot plate of food onto the coffee table ahead of us. She had not been eating. Kyle must know, despite her attempts to folly him.

Mary got up and pulled all of the blinds shut in the living room. This served to block out the sun from entering into the house through the windows. She then wrapped herself tightly within a blanket and returned to the couch.

I laid myself down next to her, my head resting on her legs. So warm was this moment of pure bliss. Perhaps the greatest joy on earth was the affectionate bonding between two souls. Even if that bond was shared on the couch, watching television, with the blinds pulled shut. The sun was not invited to our moment of adoration.

Mary dropped the television's remote control to the hardwood floor, but not until after she clicked the TV off. Though I anticipated the sound it would make, I still recoiled with a flinch.

Mary gently rubbed my face with her soft fingers. Her hand slowly moved to the underside of my neck and I began to drift off to sleep. The tears trickling from just below her eyes and down the side of her cheek made a silent kind of sound, naked to the untrained ear, but I... *I* could hear her pain. Keeping my face flat against her legs, I opened and lifted my eyes up to meet hers.

She began to sniffle. A smile, warm like the sun, peaked through her cloudy face as she suppressed her cry. She was in pain, that much I could sense long before the tears had arrived, but, in that moment, I knew she was happy. I stayed with her on the couch, by her side until she and I had both fallen asleep.

I awoke later in the day to the strange sounds of the television screaming 'buy this, look like that,' and 'feel that certain sort of way'. Though Mary was asleep, at some point she had rolled over and turned the television back on. Maybe she just wanted the company of human conversation, even if it was a one-sided fictional affair.

I do wish I could speak the language of man. While my own language is diverse and spoken through emotion, humans don't always pick up on my voice. Sam certainly had a tough time understanding me. Or maybe he just never really cared.

It startled me to see Mary's eyes move. She had been awake and I was not even aware. She was trapped in her own mind, succumbing to a certain sort of sadness. Once again, tears slowly trickled down the side of her face, and this time, I was unsure of what to do.

Slowly rolling over and jumping to the floor, I figured I would ask her to go outside. Maybe she and I going out for a walk would do her good right now. *God knows I could take a leak, anyway.*

A few minutes passed and she did not turn to see me sitting upright on the floor, staring at her for her attention. I wined and still she did not move. Placing my paw against her backside, I again complained. This time, she slowly turned to face me.

"You need to go outside?" she asked with sadness in her voice.

Yeah. Come on. We can both get out for a little bit.

Slowly, she removed the blanket that encased her like a worm that lives through the winter in a cocoon. Though Mary was a beautiful girl, she did not emerge from her cocoon a butterfly. She looked sickly and she shook as she slid on her slippers and painfully fastened her robe together.

Once outside, I handled my business and tried to catch leaves in my mouth. The wind was blowing the foliage around in all directions, which made it fun to chase after. Mary did not come outside with me, so I wasted an unknown length of time acting like a foolish puppy. I reminded myself that I was an adult and that I should get back inside and keep her company.

Heading up the steps, I barked lightly to get Mary's attention. After a moment passed by where she did not come, I began to jump up against the door in a more vigorous attempt to raise awareness to me still being outside. The window was high and it was difficult to see in. Barking and carrying on, I continued in my pleas to be heard until my legs felt sore. I had marked up the door pretty good and when Kyle got home, he would not be at all happy about it.

She probably got in the shower and forgot that I was outside. I will just go wander around a bit until she is done.

I turned to face out into the yard. The sky was getting cloudy. They were not the fun, fluffy kind of clouds either. They were the dark ones that tended to be much more violent in their ways; the ones that often came with bolts of lightning from the sky of an angry god.

A rumbling echo of madness ruptured down through the valley. The sound ran up the base of my spine and into my skull, forcing my heart to sink deep into my stomach. Like the coward that I was, I ran, dashed across the yard and down the street. I would have been safer having stayed where I was, but sometimes when you are scared you just don't think clearly. So as the thunder clashed through the sky and the rain drenched the soils of the land, I ran. Before long, I found myself taking shelter underneath a large truck. I squeezed my eyes shut as the wind picked up and howled like a thousand ferocious wolves aching to tear my throat out. I placed my head down into the mud and just tried not to think about it.

Running was a mistake. With the weather getting worse, I will have to stay put until daybreak. I did just that.

With a night full of terror-based thunder, lightning, wind, and rain, I did not sleep, but rather I sat in the mud and thought about Sam. Despite his flaws, he had never once left me out in the rain. Kyle and Mary were great people, but nothing could fill the void that Sam had left in my heart. The comfort he brought me was that of a leader to his flock. Sam was the alpha male and without him I was nothing but a coward in the mud on a cold and stormy night.

Chapter 9

Look at the Flowers

The next morning, after the storm passed, I returned home. After barking and scratching up against the door in an attempt to be heard, I concluded that neither Kyle nor Mary were there.

This time, I will stay put on the porch and wait, I thought as I sat upright against the door and looked out into the yard. The day was mostly dull as I waited for the two of them to get home. People passed me by. They walked down the street and a few squirrels played chase, but I did not give in to the temptation of running them off. I was tired, dirty, and hungry. The mud from the night before had dried into my fur, and trying to clean it was a task that kept me busy throughout the day until it turned to night.

They still are not home, I thought. *Where did they go?*

Maybe they went out looking for me. I am such a fool to have run off last night.

The air grew cold as the stars in the sky began their late-night twinkle high over the earth. The moon was bright in its ascension above. It lit up the yard in an eerie sort of way as the city fell silent and all of life retreated back inside to the comfort of their homes for an evening of slumber.

A car came to a stop on the street at the end of the driveway. A man got out and began walking up to the house as the car pulled away. With his low-hung face and slouched posture, it was hard to tell who exactly the man was. I stood up as my muscles grew tense in anticipation. The moonlight shimmered across the man's face and I was quick to realize who it was. I bolted off the porch with my tail wagging and ran up to greet my friend.

Kyle! Oh boy am I glad to see you! I wasn't sure you were going to come home, but I waited right here for you!

"Hey, Linus," Kyle said in a monotone voice.

Now near him, I could see his hair was a mess and his face was scruffy. He dripped from head to toe a sense of sadness and came off as exhausted and broken.

Sorry I didn't recognize you. You didn't even look like yourself in the darkness.

Kyle unlocked the door and allowed me to enter inside first. The house was dark and felt exceedingly cold; so much so that I had to turn and look to Kyle to be sure that the house we had entered was really even our own. After Kyle closed the door behind himself, he unloaded the contents of his pockets onto the floor. A set of car keys, cigarettes, and a lighter crashed down onto the hardwood and the sound forced me to jump.

You don't smoke.

Kyle's back hit the wall with a thud and he dropped down to his knees. His hands caught his head and he began to weep. I sat down next to him and in that moment I was slightly taller than he.

He looked up with tears in his eyes. "Hey, Linus," the words slurred out of his mouth with a breath that smelled of fire and smoke.

Hey Man, what's wrong? You know you should talk to me more, I am, after all, the world's greatest listener. I even- Kyle cut me off as he began to rub me just behind my ears and I couldn't help but wag my tail as I lost my current train of thought.

We sat in silence on the cold wooden floor for hours, until we both fell asleep where we remained on the ground.

***

That winter, Kyle and I had the entire house to ourselves. Cheshire had passed away on Christmas day, and though I was unsure where it was Mary had gone, she never returned. The way that Kyle would cry himself to sleep some nights suggested Mary was not going to ever come back. She was sick the last time I had seen her and perhaps, like Cheshire, she too had passed away, leaving a hole in Kyle's heart. He had stopped going to work and was now spending all of his time secluded and alone. It was a long and difficult winter that couldn't have ended soon enough.

Though the shades to the windows were pulled tightly closed, I soon knew that winter was dissipating away into spring. I could smell it; I could feel it. I also heard birds chirping outside. They were singing a fun sort of song as they gave praise to the change of seasons.

Kyle was sitting at the table in the kitchen. He spent the entire morning scribbling on paper with a blank and empty stare. He would occasionally crumple up his notes, then restart from scratch. I lingered near, keeping an eye on him while giving him some space to sulk in his now-routine sorrow.

The doorbell rang and I sprung over to check out who it was. Kyle slowly rolled his fingers on the table, seemingly debating whether he was going to answer the door or not.

"Come on, Man, it's Drew," pleaded the voice of a friend behind the wooden door.

Kyle rose to his feet and grabbed the papers he was fiddling with all morning. He slid them beneath a pile of books that resided on the center of the table, then he answered the door. A skinny man with a clean-shaven face entered the house. His hair was red and slicked back neatly. He had a nose so long and pointed, it could almost be considered dangerous.

"Hey Man, how are you holding up?" the man questioned as he entered and looked around. The house was mostly dark. Empty bottles littered the floor. A blanket that smelled like Mary was draped across the couch. At some point as of late, Kyle had stopped sleeping in his bed and he now slept nightly on the couch.

Kyle silently filled a pot with water and placed it onto the stove. He then sighed and turned to face our guest. "What do you want, Drew?"

"Just worried about you, Kyle. Your phone is disconnected, you don't leave the house, and no one has been able to get ahold of you since... well, you know."

"So you just thought that you would check in, make sure I hadn't killed myself yet?" Kyle pressed with intimidation in his tone.

"I didn't say that, but yeah, people are worried about you. Heard you are backed up on your mortgage, if you need help with-"

"What fucking business of yours is my life, Drew?" Kyle snapped.

Having never heard Kyle in a state of anger, I flinched in response to his uproar.

"Just get out," Kyle added softly. He didn't admit it, but I think he realized his outburst was nowhere near like himself.

"No, Kyle, I want to help you. You can't just drink your pain away like this. I-"

"I told you to get the fuck out, Drew!" Kyle flared as he picked up the tea kettle from the stove and threw it against the wall. Water rained down onto the floor and I pulled back under the table to cower.

A moment of awkward silence followed as Kyle regained control of his heavy breathing and Drew simply watched over him with a pair of disappointed eyes. For a brief second or two, the scent of murder was in the air. It was a smell I was all too keen on detecting, the scent a man gives off moments before he gives into the barbaric tendencies that beckon in his mind. If Drew didn't leave, Kyle was going to kill him. Maybe Drew could even detect this, and knew it to be true. He nodded and quietly left the house.

"Linus?" Kyle called.

I poked my head out from underneath the table and Kyle sat down on the floor with me in a puddle of water. "I am sorry," he said.

It's okay, Kyle. Sam used to get really mad sometimes, too.

***

A few months passed and I found myself in an awkward situation. I had awoken from an evening nap to find Kyle on the floor in the living room. He had the barrel of his revolver jammed into his mouth and began moaning as his tears picked up the pace in which they freely flowed down his prickly, unshaven face.

Shit... Hey, Kyle, listen, you want to go for a ride in the BMW or something?

"Ahhh!" Kyle roared with his hand trembling as he tightened his grip around the weapon.

I backed away from him, unsure of whether I was welcome or not in his presence. He then threw his revolver onto the floor like a child throwing a tantrum. The weapon slid across the ground and spun to a stop just below my feet. Kyle sunk his beat-red face into his hands and bawled himself to sleep like a man who had lost everything.

***

Kyle and I spent the next day outside. Despite me thinking that we would get out a lot more in the spring season, we never really did. An entire other season had passed of us being cooped up inside while I tried to fix Kyle's shattered mind from rotting out of his skull. Summer was here now, and with that came a warm set of rays to brighten the world around us. I figured the addition of sunshine in our lives would help alleviate the weight of trying to cheer Kyle up. It had gotten to the point where I was beginning to succumb to the sadness that lived within the house. I could not recall the last time I had seen Kyle smile, let alone laugh.

Today is the first day of the rest of our lives. Kyle and I were going to go for a ride in the convertible. It was the first time the two of us together had gone on an adventure since last fall, just before Mary had left.

Driving through the rolling hills of upstate New York with Kyle in his old German BMW was a smooth, luxurious experience. Most dogs enjoy sticking their head out of the window to feel the wind on their face, but today I had the benefit of enjoying the wind from all fronts. My ears flapped freely behind me and my cheeks rattled back.

Haha, awesome. Things are going to be different this time, I just know it.

After two seasons of misery, we, at last, were returning to life from the shadows.

With a big smile on my face and my ears flapping in the wind, I turned to face Kyle. *Hey Kyle, do you think German Shepherds get to do this all the time? Ha get it? I am so funny sometimes.*

Kyle was quiet on our drive. The sound of the universe passing us by was enough to fulfill twenty lifetimes of conversation. A certain sort of distilled oddness accompanied the two of us on our drive. I couldn't pinpoint the issue, but it felt different and strange. A blank stare filled Kyle's face and, after a few minutes of this, I realized something was very wrong.

Hey Buddy, everything OK? I repositioned myself closer to him and he began to scratch me behind my ear. Immediately after petting me, Kyle's eyes began watering up.

Okay, so something is wrong. Did I do something wrong? Where are we going?

I began to fuss about and squirm.

Kyle let out a "shhh," in an attempt to comfort me, but it did little to actually help.

We approached a large, open park with swings, slides, and children playing about. Kyle put the car in park, opened his door and ushered me out. I jumped down and sat looking up at him for the next command.

Do you want to go play ball or something?

Kyle's watery eyes began to spill over as tears slowly dripped down the side of his face. This was awful and I was unsure as to what I should do. I hung my head and began to lick his fingers, which hung down to his sides.

"It's okay, pal, you are a good dog and I love ya, Buddy, but I have something I need to go and do. You cannot come with me to do it," Kyle sniffled out.

What are you talking about I can't go with you? You are my best friend, Man!

"Who am I kidding, I doubt you even understand me... I guess it just feels better to talk out loud to you because you have been more of a friend to me than most of the human beings I have met in my life." Kyle sobbed.

I put the top of my head against his legs, looking down, I hid the hurt my heart shared with him.

"Maybe you do understand me, you always seemed good

at that, Linus."

Kyle reached into his cargo pockets, pulled out a small calcium bone and fed it to me. He then pulled out another, patted me on my head, and made sure I was locked into eye contact with the treat before he heaved it up and out into the air with all of his strength. I took off after it; I was so fast, closing in on it as it began to descend from the sky. *I bet I can catch this thing before it hits the ground. That will impress you, Kyle!*

I leaped up into the air to snag the snack, but fell short by a foot or two.

Damn, so close!

I scooped up the calcium bone, but did not eat it. *I will bring it back to Kyle and have him throw it again. One more chance and I will show him that I can be faster.*

I turned around to see Kyle's BMW turning out of the park and picking up speed as he accelerated down the road. I immediately dropped the treat he baited me with and took off after him. Running as fast I could, I took long, accurate strides; I flew around the park's outer fence and made my way onto the asphalt road.

No! Wait!

His car disappeared up over a hill, but I continued to run up after him. The pavement was beginning to burn my paws but still I continued onward. My lungs began to feel sharp and I gradually slowed down as I reached the top of the hill.

Below was a valley. The road lead down and back up over another, taller hill. I looked up to the sky and the sun. I glanced left to right to try and figure out where he had gone, where I was, and how I was to get home, but I was adrift in a sea of green hills and homes.

Kyle had vanished and it was this moment I was, again, alone in my life.

I got off the burning road and climbed up into the grass. A set of shrubs opened up to reveal a field of dandelions and I found a spot to lay among the patch of flowers.

He will come back for me; I will just wait right here for him.

Chapter 10

Freedom Is Slavery

I hid within a bed of weeds and flowers as I watched bees collect pollen from their blossoms. All afternoon, they relentlessly worked to no end. *There is no time for play when you are a bee, I suppose. It must be a full-time job caring for such a large family.* Though I sat amongst their ranks, the insects of the world paid me no mind as the sun began to set for some rest after a long hot day.

A flurry of cars passed by on the road below as families left for home after their fun-filled afternoon in the park.

I felt as though I wanted to cry and I started to dig at my right paw to take my mind off of what I refused to accept. Deeper, I gnawed and chewed until I could taste blood in my mouth. It was then that I realized that darkness had surrounded me. The moon was high and the bees were no more.

Maybe this is punishment for leaving Sam last year.

Alone in a field of emptiness, the moon was my only companion. While it was not like my breed to worship her, I wept in my sorrow and howled up to the bright, beautiful goddess in the sky. I pleaded with her for forgiveness in my wrongdoings and asked for guidance home. I just wanted to go home. She did not respond to my plea but, rather, she elegantly drifted across the sky as the night pressed on. Soon too did I find myself drifting, but I was not in the sky, I was slowly succumbing to a slumber under the stars that called the darkness above home.

***

I woke up early the next morning to watch rabbits chew away on dandelions. Their mouths rotated in a circular motion, which seemed funny to me. I began to rise up off of the cold ground, my coat slightly wet from the morning dew. The two brown rabbits froze still, with their eyes locked on me.

What do they think, if they do not move I will not see them?

I slowly continued to rise and, as soon as I was in a position to spring forward to play chase with them, they took off like little rockets zipping about the open field. I leaped after them, but every other one of their hops was a side step. Their little tails helped in misleading me the wrong way as they bounced off into the opposite direction. Master escape artists, rabbits.

They split up and I wasted no time in falling for their attempt to confuse me further. I continued on after the smaller of the two. Suddenly, before I could realize what was happening, he was circling me and as I dug my heels into the ground to turn right, he was again back in front of my original position. A marvelous play on the part of the little ball of brown fur. He was again off, this time far away into the distance.

You win this time!

Panting, I walked across the field of green, orange, and yellow to a line of pine trees. I could hear a stream of water running, hidden away through the brush below that reminded me of just how thirsty I was. I jogged up and down the line of thick shrubbery until I found an opening to the running stream. The current looked slow enough as to not take me away, and yet deep enough that I could submerge myself completely in. So I ran for it, diving high up through the air to ensure that I would make the biggest of splashes on impact. The water was cold and refreshing. I slurped away for a minute or two before paddling back to the shallow end to splash around.

I could see clusters of tiny little fish underneath me, so I took a seat in the water to get a closer look. They drifted back and forth together. When one turned left, they all turned left. When one dived lower, they all followed suit. This is what family is, and while Kyle turned right and I followed, when I stopped he did not. While I considered him family, the harsh truth was he did not feel the same of me. I wondered what Mary would have thought of Kyle leaving me the way that he had, but who was she to judge?

I got out of the water and shook the wetness from my fur. The morning air was chilly. Maybe jumping into the river so early on in the day was a bad idea in hindsight.

I walked up a hill consisting of mostly rocky terrain, which dug a bit into my paws. The bits of sharp rock were painful, but did not puncture the skin or draw blood, so I continued hiking up until reaching the very top, which paid off with a breathtaking view for miles in all directions. An endless array of hills dipped into one another as far as I could see. Some reached so high that they could touch up into the clouds. As far as I was concerned, it was quite an impressive feat for mounds of motionless grass and dirt to be touching the clouds like they were.

Down in the valley below were fields of corn and

meadows of tall thick grass. It was an incredible feeling to be up so high on top of the world as I then knew it. To be awarded the opportunity to witness the sea of plant life below sway in the breeze that blew in from the west was as close to a feeling of enlightenment than I had ever previously reached.

The taste of the open, fresh air was marvelous. I could live out in the countryside with a life of solitude for the rest of my days if only I were not so hungry. I have never had to hunt and catch my own food. All my life, I have relied on others to feed me. Now, being alone in the world, I was forced to realize that I was ignorant in the ways of my forefathers. Their means of survival were something I had never known. It was something that was lost over the years in the domestication of my species. Somewhere in the process of befriending man, we gave up who we were to become man's pet. We lost ourselves in becoming submissive to an alpha male no more deserving of the title than the moles digging holes in the fields below me.

How exactly did that happen?

The breeze shifted directions and, with it, came the distinct scent of something to eat. I made way down the hill and dropped my nose to the ground in order to track down the source of the smell.

After a minute or two I had found what I was looking for. It was the carcass of a chipmunk, or at least what was left of it. The meat had been all but picked clean by other scavengers. A trail of ants in a perfect line were quickly stripping away what was left of the meat. So, my first order of business, if I wanted to dine on this cuisine, was to pick up what was left of it and take it away from the ants.

Making haste, I grabbed the body and sprinted a bit further down the hill until I was sure I was well enough away from the ants to enjoy my meal. A few had made it into my mouth, which forced me to shake my head around like some crazed turkey who had lost his mind. I yacked up a bit. It's a creepy feeling to have ants crawling around in your mouth.

I looked down at what was left of the chipmunk and wasted very little time diving right in. It wasn't so much that the carcass was tasty by any means, but rather it was something to eat. Given that the very last time I had ingested a meal was the biscuit Kyle tossed in order to deceive me so that he may abandon me, I was famished.

Like some wild beast, I ripped and picked at my meal, focusing on it and it alone as I scraped the bones clean.

I caught something moving just out of the corner of my eye. It was a chipmunk. This one was alive and well, standing directly ahead of me. It had maneuvered against the strains of grass that blew a particular direction with the wind. That was the single costly mistake that allowed me to notice it.

I froze as I calculated just how best to go about slaughtering the rodent. As it looked into my eyes, I realized that this chipmunk was not fearful for its life. It wasn't frozen in place because it thought that standing still would be the best tactic to use for me to not see him; it was frozen in stature due to shock. It was locked into a type of mourning. Its eyes poured forth a certain kind of sadness that I had seen countless times before. When living with Kyle and Mary, I had seen this particular look of sorrow.

I glanced down to the corpse I had indiscreetly ripped apart and then back up to the chipmunk watching over me. I had made a mess of its friend and I found myself stuck in one of the more awkward situations I had ever been within. I simply licked the corpse once or twice apologetically, attending to an open wound I had not intended to create. But the wounds of this deceased 'munk were far beyond means of curation. It was dead and I was folly to think I could simply eat a meal in such a disrespectful way. Not knowing of any other way to say I am sorry, I simply stood up and walked away. I passed by the chipmunk who was still frozen in his look of absolute horror and disgust.

There was an opening in the tree line, which allowed me

to see again clearly into the lowlands. The wind was chilly, but tasted refreshing. I closed my eyes, took a deep breath, and listened to the wind as it bounced between the hills. It howled out to me in an ancient language I longed to understand. After partaking in a moment of spiritual bliss, I opened my eyes and spotted a farm to the far side of a cornfield that claimed much of the valley below. Descending the rest of the way down the hill to investigate, I entered in through the field of towering stalks. It would be far too easy to get lost in this intricate labyrinth of vegetables. I used the sun as a compass and kept it positioned just over my left shoulder as I pressed on through the great maze.

Thanks in part to my clever navigational tactics, I was through the corn field just as soon as I had entered, or at least it felt that fast. I had made it just outside the heart of the farm.

The ranch consisted of a few buildings. There was a little house with a wrap-around porch and a long dirt driveway that connected to the road. There was a barn that towered over the house and a fairly large shed that sat comfortably between the two. A couple hundred yards behind the barn and the house were a line of small stables.

A fence was to my right. Startled, I jumped backwards after noticing a giant hooved beast was glaring down at me from the other side of the wire fence. It was a horse and, when I leaped in fear, so too did it. I don't think it was afraid of me, but the chain reaction of me being startled in turn started it. *Where did you come from?* The horse was a magnificent, muscular creature of brown color with a long, black mane. I don't think there was an inch of fat on his chiseled frame. He was fit through and through.

I playfully barked at the horse twice, then dropped to the ground in a pouncing position. He gave me a loud nay and took off down alongside the fence. I sprung up after it and, even though there was a fence in between the two of us, we played chase.

The horse would slow down just enough for me to catch up, then off like a rocket it blew past me. Again and again, I barked and ran but was no such match for this champion of speed. I slowed down, panting as I struggled to inhale large gasps of air. I was a sprinter, but this horse was a marathon runner.

And to think, I thought it was the creatures smaller than I that were faster. This beast could smoke even the fastest of squirrels.

A high pitched whistle echoed from the cluster of stables and the horse galloped away.

Great, he left me.

I dropped down into the tall grass to disguise myself and began an investigation into the source of the sound. The whistle had come from a shirtless man who was scanning over the horizon.

He must have heard me barking and playing with the horse.

Staying silent, I gave him no cause to investigate further, and so he returned to his work inside the large shed.

A black truck slowly approached up the long driveway of dirt. It left behind a trail of dust that looked like a swarm of apocalyptic locusts. The truck stopped just outside of the shed, and a heavyset man with a pot belly got out. He began speaking to the guy that was inside, but I was too far away to hear what it was they were saying. I pressed through the field of tall grass until at last making it to the more comfortable lower-cut stuff.

The amount of heat these tall meadows maintain is intense. Makes trekking through it all the more exhausting.

Making my way down to the shed, I engaged stealth mode and crept my way into a position where I could see and listen to the heavyset man. Though I stayed out of eyesight, I was close enough to see who he was conversing with. It was a skinnier man, the one who had whistled at me. He was wearing dark-colored cargo shorts that matched the tan of his shirtless chest. He looked to be crafting items; belts, bags, and straps of various lengths with a set of raw materials.

Perhaps leather?

A very loud, unsettling sound echoed from out of the fenced-in meadow. It raised the hairs on the back of my neck and wasn't quite like anything I had ever heard before.

"Tess is still crying, I hear," said the heavyset man. "How long has she been at it?"

"On and off all week... though it's been more on than off," the shirtless man said as he put down his tools and picked up a cloth to wick away the sweat that poured from his face.

"Sad when you gotta separate a calf away from its mother," said the big guy.

"Yeah, It's tough, but we have no use for a male calf and we need Tess's milk to make up for last year," the skinny man said as he tossed the cloth aside and put a button up shirt on over his bare skin.

"Still trying to recover from that eco tax, eh?"

"Things have been tense around here. Just trying to make ends meet, you know? Stace got a second job, which is an idea I'm not fond of, but her income from teaching goes almost entirely to our mortgage alone."

"Yeah, everybody is struggling."

"Not all over, just us that live under the poverty line. Everyone above us seems to be flourishing just fine at our expense," the skinny guy complained in a groaning tone. "Regardless, John," he added before pausing to pat the larger man on the shoulder, "I appreciate you coming out here on your day off to lend me a hand."

Politics. Why human beings think they can enslave one another with mind games and money is a sick concept that I cannot bear to listen to for a moment longer.

"Mhmm. You bet, Mitch. Me and Ann will do anything we can for you guys. You know that."

I left my vantage point and went out to seek the source of

the odd sound I had heard. Just as soon as I had, the sound again echoed from one of the fields nearby.

A wire fence blocked my path. It radiated with the sound of electricity, so I carefully squeezed under. All was well until about halfway through when my backside rubbed up against a strand of the cable. My entire body was violently stunned and shocked. I squealed in pain and quickly clawed forward the rest of the way.

My heart was racing as I turned back to look at the wretched fence. There were sharp strands of the electrified wire that had torn a patch of my fur from my backside when I got stuck.

That really hurt.

Again, I heard the chilling cry. It was coming from the stables nearby. I slowly approached and popped my head into one of the stables to look around. Hay littered the floor of the dark room where a large white cow with black spots stood in the corner.

Oh wow, a cow!

Again the cow cried a heart-wrenching moan of misery as I approached. Ruffling through the hay, I captivated the attention of the large bovine. It turned to face me with a facial expression that embodied its sadness. I couldn't be sure if the cow were at all emotionally together.

You must be the cow those men were talking about. I believe they called you Tess. Tess is your name, right?

The cow glanced down at me with its big brown eyes as if peering past my skin and fur to see directly into the core of my soul. I wanted to feel uneasy at first, being so close to such a large beast - cows are much bigger in person than they appear on the television - but my insecurities were quickly suppressed by the welcoming sense of warmth the cow seemed to radiate. I do not mean this in a physical manner, rather this cow, with its soft eyes, seemed to be pulling me in. It pleaded with me to stay and rest; talk and listen awhile; so I did just that.

I'm Linus.

Though I had never conversed with a cow, I quickly gathered that the body language of such an animal was very similar to that of a dog. I slowly approached and stopped only when I was close enough that advancing any further may make the cow feel uncomfortable. She was hurt; not physically, but emotionally. I could see her pain as it poured from the expressions of her soul. So, sitting upright, I gazed again into her eyes. For close to an hour we kept each other company and communicated in silence.

The sounds of violently thick vibrations rattled through my skull. I perked my head up to look around for the source of the distinct sound. The perpetrator was a hummingbird, who dipped down to briefly observe both Tess and I before teleporting away to carry on with its day.

Did you know hummingbirds use spider silk to put the finishing touches on their nest? It's true, I saw it on the television once when I lived with Mary and Kyle.

The thought of my two friends, now gone, dampened my spirits, but I continued on with my blabbering to the cow. She was a fantastic listener.

I hate spiders. Courageous little guys, them hummingbirds, to be stealing web from a spider and such.

A cold draft blew into the stables.

I popped my head out to see that the day had begun its shift into dusk. The setting sun illuminated the sky an eerie sort of red. As its final moments of shining slowly ticked away, so too did the warmth that it cast down upon the land.

It will be dark soon. Awkward question, but do you mind if I stay in here with you tonight?

Tess stepped towards me and slowly laid herself down in a pile of the hay. She began licking my face with her long, scratchy tongue.

Hey, knock that off.

Honestly, though, I didn't mind. Her presence was

comforting as darkness staked its claim to reside over the world.

***

The next morning, I woke up to find myself snug up against Tess. She was so warm and it was comforting to have been granted her company throughout the coldness of the night. She was awake long before me and she was just sitting there peacefully, looking at me with her big, soft eyes. With my stomach grumbling and aching, I squirmed to my feet.

Listen, I'm really hungry. I am going to go see if I can't find us some food. I will bring you back some, OK?

Tess just stared at me with her consistent, saddened look. I wanted to comfort her, and I figured bringing her food was something that I could do to satisfy both her and me. Taking my leave from her stable, I made way for the electrified fence. As to not get shocked this time, I dug a deep hole below the lowest hanging wire. This gave me plenty of clearance for my backside to avoid the wire as I crawled underneath it.

Guided with my nose, I made way for the house near the road where I found two trashcans. I threw my body weight into one and it came tumbling over with a thud. The lid popped off on impact and the contents of the can flew out into the dirt.

Alright, let's see what could smell so good as to catch my attention from so far.

I rummaged through the trash and found some traces of honey mustard, ketchup, and even bread buried within less appealing additions that I would pass on. I licked up the edibles that I found until I found what it was that had smelled so good. It was a whole turkey! Sort of. It was mostly picked clean down to the bones, but there were definitely some scraps and ligaments still intact that pleaded with my stomach to be consumed. I grabbed hold of the bird with my mouth and ventured on back to the stables to share my find with Tess.

As a truck pulled up alongside the house, I dove off into a

ditch as to not be seen. In doing so, I dropped the turkey on the gravel of the driveway. As the truck pulled to a stop, an old man got out and the shirtless man who I had seen the day before came out of his house to greet his guest. He was fully dressed and I then put the pieces together that he was the farmer who laid claim over this land.

"Nicholas," the farmer welcomed.

"Morning, Mitch," the old man said in a low voice. It sounded familiar, and yet I couldn't place it.

I have to get that turkey and get out of here, I thought. But I knew that if I got up from the ditch, the two of them would see me and my gig would be over before it had really even started.

"Listen, Nicholas, we can reschedule. I don't-"

"Nonsense," the old man groaned in his soft tone, cutting the farmer off mid-sentence.

"Well, Nicholas, I am sorry; Stacey and I both are. If you need anything, you just holler."

"Well, I appreciate that, Mitch. Funeral is scheduled for the Saturday after next if you and Stacey would like to attend. I know that would mean a lot to us," the older man explained. "Nothing can compare to the feeling of hurt after losing a boy, but going to work helps take my mind off things. I had made arrangements with you prior to vaccinate these here horses, and I intend to keep 'em. Never backed down on my word; not going to start now."

I shifted my body around in the ditch to get a better look on the two. I could see the farmer clearly, but the older man had his back to me.

The farmer, Mitch, curled his lips inward and nodded. "Okay, Nicholas. Well, I appreciate you being here and, if there is anything myself or Stace can do for ya, you best be sure to let us know."

"I will. Thank you,"

"The hell is that?" Mitch said as his gaze was captured by

the turkey I had dropped in the gravel. He raised his eyebrows and the older man who was with him turned to look as well. It was then that I realized where it was I had recognized the old man's gentle tone from. He was Kyle's father: the veterinarian who had patched me up.

It is now or never, I thought as the two men started to walk over to investigate why exactly the carcass of a cooked turkey lay in the driveway.

I sprung forward from the ditch and latched my jaw around the turkey before bolting off across the field.

"Hey, what the hell!" the farmer shouted at me as I claimed the scraps as my own. Kyle's father furrowed his bushy eyebrows and stuck his arm out in front of the farmer to halt him from chasing after me. The two simply stood and watched as I bolted off into the field of tall grass.

I ran until I was out of breath. I knew just how crucial it was to put some distance between myself and them if I didn't want to get caught. After I stopped, I turned around to ensure that they were not following me. It was hard to tell through the sea of tall grass, but I knew that they had not followed me into the meadow. I doubled back and crawled under the electric fence, then I snuck into the stable where Tess was still resting on the ground.

Tess, look! I found a turkey for us!

I set the bird down in front of her and allowed her to eat first... Tess simply looked at me, as if confused.

Are you not hungry? Or maybe you just do not like to eat turkey... Oh, I feel stupid... you probably do not even eat birds.

Tess licked the side of my face as if she were thanking me for the offer anyway. She then looked at me with her big, puffy eyes as if suggesting I go on ahead without her.

Well, if you are sure.

I looked down to my catch and gave it a whiff. It had been in the trash overnight, but it still smelled phenomenal. Especially given how hungry I was. I dug in and spent the next hour

cleaning each and every bone dry of any and all meat. It was
only when I noticed Tess staring at me did I stop. There was
nothing left on the bird's skeleton and I had been gnawing away
at the bones for far too long. While Tess didn't judge me, I felt
barbaric and unclean. I hopped up and left the scraps so that I
could converse with my friend.

Do you want to go outside?

The cow slowly got up and came to meet me in the
center of the stable where she began cleaning the side of my
face with her scratchy tongue.

Come on, let's get out of here.

I poked my head out of the stable. The coast was clear
and I exited out into the sun-filled day. Tess followed me out
and squinted her eyes in reaction to the brightness of the sky.

As the early afternoon set in, the temperature in the air
scorched the ground, withering the grass and a row of
sunflowers across the other side of the fence. As it got hotter,
the air began to stink a foul sort of stench. It smelled like rotting
feces, and I soon noticed it was, in fact, just that. Heaps of dung
littered the field and gave the air an unfathomable wretchedness
to its smell. *How did I not notice that yesterday? I mean, I
smelled it but not like this!*

Kyle's father's truck was gone from the driveway and the
farmer who owned this property was nowhere in sight. Tess and
I wondered around the field together. The electrified wire
restricted where it was we could go. Though I could sneak
underneath it, Tess could not; so I shared in her burden of being
caged into this field of fecal matter.

*You know, Tess, I know of a place not all too far from
here where the wind is refreshing and the scene is peaceful. It is
high above in the clouds on the very top of a mountain nearby. It
would only take us a day to reach. We could run away and live
there. If I dedicate some time digging underneath the fence, I
think that I can create a hole deep enough for you to sneak
under with me.*

I dashed over to the fence and got straight to work. Tess came up behind me and laid herself down. She watched with a faint smile on her face as I dug the afternoon away.

Before I knew it, I was covered in dirt and mud. The hole was coming along nicely, but I was exhausted and, with the sun now down to sleep for the day, the air was surprisingly cold.

Should we go back to the stable and get some sleep? I think if we wake up early enough in the day, we can come out here, finish up, and set out for the top of the mountain.

Tess stood up and together we walked back to her stable. Once inside, I flopped over onto my side. I was completely exhausted. My paws and shoulders ached from an afternoon of digging for hours on end. Tess laid herself down beside me and began cleaning my fur from the dirt and mud with her tongue. In doing so, she was also massaging my sore muscles.

Ah, thanks, that feels nice.

No sooner than I finished my thought did I fall to sleep.

***

The next morning, I woke up to the sound of someone approaching the stable. I was nestled up against Tess, who was still asleep with her head against mine. As someone crept closer to the barn door, my body grew stiff, and I broke my stillness to jump to my feet. This woke up Tess, but it didn't startle her. I bolted to the back of the of the stable and stowed away behind some thick wooden beams that were shrouded in darkness.

The farmer came inside. He was carrying an old tin bucket.

"Come on, Tess, on your feet," he instructed.

The cow shakily got up with a groan.

The farmer unhooked a small wooden stool that was hanging on the wall and took a seat beside Tess's belly. He dragged his bucket against the ground and placed it directly under her udders. He then wrapped his fingers around her privates and began squeezing and pulling on them.

"Come on, Tess," he said, still fondling with her nipples.

A few minutes passed of him groping her, then he let out a sigh and stood up. Shaking his head, he picked up his empty tin bucket, grabbed the wooden stool, placed it on the hook in the wall, and then left the stable.

After I was sure that he was gone, I came out into the open.

That was awkward. Does he always do that to you?

Tess lowered her head and began licking my face.

Hey, cut that out. We have a long day ahead of us.

With the fur on my face now wet and messy, I pulled back to lick my paw and try to attend to the uncomfortable mess.

Listen, I am going to go find some breakfast and then finish up digging. I will be right back, OK?

Tess simply looked at me with her big brown eyes.

I will take that as a yes.

I poked my head outside of the stable door and ensured that the farmer was gone. After confirming the coast was clear, I sprinted down and across the field over to the house.

I dropped down underneath the electric fence and pressed my way up alongside the house. I could smell fresh scraps in the trash. With my eyes on the target, I jumped up against one of the cans. It felt heavier than it had yesterday, but even so, the trashcan tumbled over with ease. A block of concrete had been placed on the lid to keep intruders out, but that did nothing to stop me. I reached into the can for the new bag of trash and tugged it out, but froze when I heard human voices. One of the house windows was open and two people were inside talking.

Did they hear me?

"Tess still isn't producing milk?" a woman asked.

"Yeah, it's the damndest thing, usually these cows

produce more milk after giving birth, not less," responded the voice of the farmer.

"Yeah, that is odd."

"It's almost as if she is rebelling against us for taking her calf away."

"Oh, come on now, that's ridiculous."

"Aye, I know, but I have no other explanation for it."

Okay, so they didn't hear me.

I grabbed hold of the trash can and tore it open. When Sam had left us, we were forced to eat from the trash for a while. After that moment in my life, I said that never again would I ever stoop so low as to eat from the garbage; yet there I was, doing it again. I was digging through unwanted goods with hopes to find any form of minute scrap so that I may satisfy my malnourished body.

After eating some strange-smelling slop, I sneaked my way back under the fence and over to Tess's hideout. I peeked my head inside to see that she was fast asleep.

I will go finish digging the hole on my own and let her rest up for the journey ahead of us. I made way for the hole and jumped down into it. After a good night's rest, I felt ready to conquer this project and free my friend. I dug the morning away until I found myself in a hole so deep that I could barely get out of it.

This should be deep enough for Tess to squeeze under.

Covered in dirt, I went back to the stable and was greeted by a now awake Tess. She looked at me with a bit of joy in her eyes for me having returned.

Our escape plan is in motion!

Hearing footsteps behind me, I bolted to the back of the room and hid once more behind the wooden support beams.

The farmer entered the stable and approached Tess. He gently patted the cow on the top of her head, then he went on to escort her outside. I carefully made my way over to the door so that I could continue to observe.

"I'm sorry, girl, just gonna get better use out of ya dead than alive."

Out of nowhere, his relaxed demeanor intensified as he grabbed her head and jerked it off to the side. He unholstered a thick blade and quickly slid it across her tightened neck. While she struggled, Tess let out a moan of terror that was cut short with the wound that split her neck wide open.

I raised my cheeks and began to lightly growl as I flared my teeth. Without wasting another second, I jumped out from where I was hiding and latched onto the man's arm.

Filled with anger and hatred, I sank my teeth in as far as I could while he flailed around like a helpless chicken against my might. Dropping the blade he was holding into a pile of hay, he used both hands to fling me off. I sailed through the air and crashed into the outside wall of the stable. It broke as I fell to the ground, but I ignored the pain of impact and got back up.

The farmer wrapped the fingers of his left hand around the large, open wound that was on his right arm. I had done some damage. Though it was not enough to incapacitate the man, I had certainly gotten his attention.

I continued exposing my teeth and growling like a maniac. Slowly, I positioned myself between the man and Tess. The fur of my paws stepped into a warm puddle of sticky blood, and with this, I was emotionally subdued. My anger dissipated as I turned to look into the eyes of my fallen friend. She was still alive and struggling to breathe on the ground, despite her open, bleeding neck.

No, Tess, get up.

I whined and licked the side of her face.

Please, Tess. You have got to get up.

Her eyes closed and my cries became sporadically intensified

Get up, Tess, we are supposed to get out of here. You and me. I will take you to the top of the hill and you will be okay.

She was dead.

I turned back to the man who had murdered her. He looked at me with an open-mouthed expression of confusion as he continued clenching his wounded arm.

Slowly, he backed away and left me with my now dead friend.

As much as I wanted retribution, there was no fight left in me. I was defeated.

I pressed my face up against Tess's neck, which continued to drain her dead body of all the blood she stored inside. I dropped down to the ground to lay by her motionless side and cried myself to sleep.

Chapter 11

Damaged Goods

Not long after leaving me to cradle my now dead friend, the farmer had returned. He approached the stable with a baseball bat held high above his head. He had taken his shirt off and wrapped it around his bloody, injured arm. His eyes flared with anger as they drifted down to meet mine. Though he had come back to the stable with intentions in his heart of ending my life just as he had done to Tess, he was stuck in a moment of contemplation. I cared not, either way; there was no fight left in me, only sorrow and acceptance of my shadowy, gruesome fate.

The flame in the farmer's eyes fizzled out with his facial expression of anger and hatred. He dropped the bat and knelt down to the ground, then he slowly reached towards me. He must have seen that my demeanor and expression were no longer that of a fighter and he responded with sympathy.

"Ah, shit," he groaned. He then picked me up and carried me outside. I hung my head down in the air and looked back into Tess's cold, lifeless eyes. The image of her lying on the floor, dead, in a pool of her own blood was a thought that would serve to haunt me for the rest of my days.

The farmer placed me in a large, wooden crate, which is where I stayed throughout the afternoon. He draped a large towel over the top of my prison so that I could not be granted the freedom of vision. The temperature dropped and soon the air became frigid. I huddled in the corner as darkness set in and soon everything was black. The towel insured that my night was spent alone. No stars, no moon, and no clouds would keep me company on this night. I tried my best to ignore the cries of my consciousness; it sought only to frighten me further and belittle my mind amidst my helpless scenario.

Why didn't he just kill me, too, I cynically thought as I shivered the night away while thinking of Tess in her final seconds of life.

***

The next morning, I heard the voices of two men conversing as they approached my sheathed crate.

"Some of the best cops go out eating the barrel of their own gun. It's a fucking tragedy, but I don't blame him. Not after what he went through."

"Yeah, I guess he just couldn't go on without Mary. Between losing her and being suspended from work and all, it was just too much. But even so, nothing could ever be so bad as to justify ending it all, eh?" questioned the farmer, who I could not see. Both of the men were now standing just beside the crate.

"Well, until you are in those shoes, you just will never know," the second man said. I quickly picked up on where I had heard his voice before. He was the heavyset man who had come to speak with the farmer on the first day that I had arrived on the farm. "So, what is the deal with this here dog, now?" he added, trying to uplift the mood of their conversation away from its current dark stance and towards the task at hand.

The farmer tore the blanket free from over the crate and I was quickly blinded by the light of the rising sun. I had lived in a state of complete darkness for almost an entire day. My eyes stung as I blinked them amid the brightness of day.

"Well, look at you," the big guy said with a smile as he perched down to inspect me. "Handsome little fellow, aren't you?"

"Almost beat the damn thing to death when it bit me yesterday. Little fucker got me good," the farmer added as he lifted his bandaged arm. "Anyway, Nichols came by the other day to vaccinate the horses and, as it turns out, he recognized this here dog. I guess Kyle had originally found it starving to death in that house with all them dead girls. His partner had shot it and Nichols had operated on the little mutt. Saved his life, then Kyle kept it. Said the dog was sweet as can be, kept Mary company right to the very end."

"But you said it bit you," the heavy man pointed out.

"Yeah, well, I think it had grown a little too attached to Tess before we slaughtered her is all."

"Ah, that makes sense." The big guy poked his fat fingers into my cage and rubbed at my face, just below the eyes. "You just needed a friend, didn't ya'? You sure have been through a lot."

"So," the farmer continued. "With me being suspended and the truck's tags being no good thanks to the good folks at the New York State DM-fuckin'-V, I can't be out on the road. Was wondering if you would take him over to the shelter."

"Yeah, I can do that," the big guy agreed as he kept his gaze locked into mine. His facial expression became sad and for a moment I felt as though both he and I understood each other. "Surprised you didn't call Mitch for this one."

"Well, his son did just eat the barrel of a gun. I figured I shouldn't be calling him about a stray," the farmer pointed out coldly.

The big guy slowly nodded and said nothing.

"Don't say anything about him biting me, though, or else they will put him down."

"Well, unless someone adopts him, they will put him down anyway."

An awkward silence lingered in the air after the bleak statement was made. It felt all too familiar, like the stagnant fragrance of a dead corpse on the ground. Then the heavy guy broke the silence by unbolting the wooden locks that bound the prison shut.

"Hey there, Guy. My name is John," the big guy introduced himself as he reached in towards my collar. "And you would be?" He had to pause for a moment as he strained his eyes to read the tag under my neck. Though I could not see it myself, I figured it was scratched up, thus making it difficult to read. "Linus," he finally added. "Well, come on out, Linus," he welcomed.

I hesitated at first, but then figured that they would force me out of the crate one way or another, so I crawled my way out by myself.

"Got a bit of a limp there, doesn't he?" the big guy, John, pointed out.

"Yeah... It would seem so," the farmer confirmed.

Probably due to you throwing me through a wall.

"Suppose we don't need a leash, then," John added.

Typically, I would think of something clever to say in regard to my hatred of leashes but, in that moment, I didn't really care. Hell, I didn't care for much of anything. I was ready to die hours ago; what difference was a cable tied up to my neck?

"Alright, let's get to it," John suggested as he stood up

and gave the farmer a nod. "I will see you tomorrow night, Mitch. Finished milling your AK, so I have to drop that off.

"Yeah, no rush," the farmer eased as he stared down at me. "Thanks again for taking him off my hands, John."

"It's no problem," the big guy reassured as he walked away. I understood that I was to follow him, so I did. He didn't have to twist my paw to get me to do so, either. Though I wanted to find Tess and say goodbye, I knew that the gesture would fall on a set of deaf ears. Now I just wanted to get as far away from that farm as I could.

We approached a black truck and John opened the passenger side door. "You need help get-" he cut himself off mid-sentence as I leaped up into the truck and sat upright on the seat.

John closed the door, then went around to the other side of the truck and got in. He looked over to me before starting up the truck and pulling out of the driveway. Despite being locked into a state of looking forward, my attention was adrift. The focus within the lenses of my eyes were blurred as the colors and shapes of the outside world passed us by. In that moment, my mind was both a bottle filled to the brim with an overabundant hazy liquid and an empty slate. I was nobody. I served no purpose and I had no future.

The sounds of hundreds, perhaps even thousands of dogs screeched through the air and I blinked my eyes for the first time in a while. After a long car ride, the particular length of which I could not be sure of, we had arrived at our destination. Parked, we were facing a large cement building with thin corridors like wings that branched off to the sides. Even with the windows of the truck tightly closed, I could still hear the frightening screams of the dogs who were caged within the building's thick cement walls.

John let out a loud sigh, then turned to look at me. I was still locked into my dead stare out the front window, but I could see him with my peripheral vision. He placed his hand on my neck and slowly ruffled through my fur. "You don't deserve this," he added with disappointment in his tone.

Maybe I do. Maybe I deserve all of this.

Two scrawny kids in their late teenage years exited the building. They were dressed in green suits. Using two separate thick chords, they dragged a large rottweiler around the backside of the building. The rott' dug his feet into the ground and tried to flail his body around in protest for where it was they were going.

They are taking him away to die, I thought. Despite there not being much evidence to support my claim, the fear in a dog's eyes when he sees death is exactly what that rottweiler harbored on his face. It was the expression of complete and utter terror. *I will be sure to go easy into the night. No sense in fighting it.*

John removed his hand from my head and ran it through his thinning-out blond hair. He took a deep breath, then sat in silence for a moment. After collecting his thoughts, he placed his fingers around the truck's keys that still sat idle in the ignition. He turned them and restarted the truck before turning around and pulling back out onto the road.

For the first time since being in the truck, I moved my head. I turned to look over to John, who now had his eyes on the road and his brows furrowed as if deep in thought.

What are you doing?

He must have heard my silent question as he glanced his head towards me while keeping his eyes on the road to drive. "I am going to figure something out for you, Guy," he eased as he pet me on the head with one hand and continued to steer the car with the other. His face still harbored a look of deep consideration of the options before him.

***

After driving for close to an hour, we pulled up to a little brick house nestled in between two larger ones. They towered and cast shadows over the smaller home as if laughing over just how tiny and insignificant it was for the little house to be placed within their grand world.

John leaned over and scratched my neck. "This is a good family, an old friend from work and her son. He is slightly autistic but you won't judge him, now will ya, Boy?"

Autistic? I am not familiar with such a term.

The man exited the truck. What a relief for the truck's suspension *that* must have been as it shifted back to an even estate.

"You stay right here," he suggested as he walked up the driveway.

Yeah, I am really gonna get far, locked inside of this truck.

Halfway up the driveway, he stopped, came back, and opened my door.

"Actually, it's probably best if you come along. First impressions are important," he added with a smile.

Together we walked up to the door, or rather, he walked up to the door and I limped behind. He pushed in the button for the doorbell and together we waited for an answer. After no response, he knocked on the door and chuckled. "Forgot the bell doesn't work."

A tall, thin, attractive woman answered the door. She had a tired expression with dark circles around her eyes. She had black hair and a long, pretty face.

"Hey, John, come on in."

"I didn't wake you, did I?"

"Na, pulled a double last night, but no time for sleep. Got stuff to do around the house before Charlie gets home," she said, turning her backside to us so that she may continue with whatever it was she was working on before answering the door. She stopped and came back to us, realizing slowly that I was accompanying her friend John on her doorstep.

"Who is this Cutie?" she asked, kneeling down to scratch my face. Her voice was seductively appealing, like perhaps she had perfected the art of vocal expression to get by previously in life.

"Well, this here is Linus," John introduced.

"Aww, why hello, Linus," she said, smiling from cheek to cheek.

"He is a super friendly dog looking for a family."

Her smile faltered into something sad and disappointed and she rose to her feet.

"John, I can barely take care of my kid let alone add a dog into the mix."

"Oh come on, Layla. It's not difficult. You feed him, water him, and let him outside when he asks to go pee," John declared. "It's not like a puppy where you need to train it or anything."

"I am rarely home with work, John, you know that. I don't want to come home to a dog having pissed all over my house."

Piss in the house? Come on, who do you think I am, Lady.

"He is an older dog, Layla, they can hold it in, and besides, you know Charlie would love him!"

I was sitting upright, looking up to both the man and woman with concern on my face as they talked of my fate as if I had no choice in the matter. The man reached down to ease my worry. He rubbed my nose, and I would be lying if I said I did not enjoy it.

"Apparently he has been drifting around for a while, spent some time at my cousin Mitch's farm. Befriended a cow that was sentenced to slaughter and got a little too attached. I can't take him; God knows we have *way* too many cats to throw a dog into the mix. If I drop him off to the pound, they will just put him down. My cousin advertised that he found him, but no one claimed him."

She looked down at me and frowned. "Charlie *could* use

a friend right now... that's for sure... He is just having such a tough time making any at school. Those kids can be so cruel sometimes."

The man tried to uplift the conversation, which was embarking off into a land of sadness. "Listen, didn't you have a dog when you were a kid? I remember my first dog, a shih tzu named Terry. Kids would laugh at it because shih tzu sounds like shit zoo. I know all about kids being mean to one another. Regardless, I loved that fuckin' dog. He was one of the best friends I ever had, and that statement still holds true even to this day. That dog would greet me when I got home and sleep at the foot of my bed when it was time for me to close my eyes. He would be up and at it in the mornings when I got up and he would never sleep in past me. He always had to be by my side." The big guy furrowed his brow as his moment of nostalgia induced him into a euphoric headspace. He then smiled and rubbed my head. "I'm not sure what type of breed he is. A small retriever mutt with a bit of dasch in him from the looks of it. And if that's the case, retrievers are proven companions time and time again. They are loyal to the very end."

Layla scanned me over and sighed. Her eyes met mine and, for a brief moment, I could see into her. She lived a life of struggle and concern; pain and exhaustion.

"Okay, fine," she said, caving into his sales pitch. "But the first bag of dog food is on you. I am totally broke until payday," she bargained.

The man's chubby face lit up with joy. He gripped his belt to prevent his pants from sagging as he kneeled down to look into my face. "See, told ya I would find you a good home," he said while scruffing up the hair atop my head once more.

My eyes looked past him to the setting sun out the window. Given the new angle of the sun, shadows took the opportunity to linger into the room that we resided within. The absence of light brought a chill that reminded me that the season of summer was at an end and fall was upon us. That meant that, in turn, winter was again approaching.

The two conversed for some time while I sat staring out the window.

I guess this is my new home, or at least it is until this lady decides it best to discard me like unwanted table scraps.

The large fellow gave me one final pat on the head and then took his leave from the house. This left me in the awkward situation of looking up to Layla, who fired back a gaze that suggested she were equally uncomfortable.

"So," she said with a forced smile.

It was clear that the pain I felt in my heart, she too felt, though I was unsure as to who or what exactly was the curator of her sadness.

"Charlie should be home soon," she added with raised cheeks. "He is just going to love you."

Love, huh. I doubt that.

Layla went into the kitchen and I followed. She withdrew a bowl from a cupboard and then went on to fill the dish up with tap water.

"Thirsty?" she asked as she placed the bowl down on the floor in front of me.

I reached down and slurped up most of the water. With slobber dripping from my face, I looked back up to Layla to see what was next. This forced a gentle smile on her face.

Layla left the kitchen and took a seat at the table in the dining room. She began tapping away at an old mechanical typewriter. Each stroke forced my ears to twitch in retaliation to the estranged sound. Unsure as to what I should be doing with my time, I sat by her side and just looked out of the window. The trees had begun changing the colors of their leaves. Some of the blades were brown and others yellow. A few of the leaves had even started their migration towards death. Gracefully, they drifted through the air and down to the ground. I began counting them as I pressed my face up against the window to further my focus, but I lost track when a big yellow bus pulled up to a stop in front of the house.

A little boy wearing an awkwardly large backpack exited the bus and waddled up to the steps of the house. The doorknob to the home began to slowly turn and Layla stopped what she was doing. She stood up and walked to the door so that she could greet her son as he entered into the house.

The boy was very small and looked silly trying to push his way inside. He had a thin face, messy black hair, and pasty white skin. The kid looked like an awkward miniature version of his mother.

"A doggy," the boy pointed out, laying eyes on me. As he drew near, I noticed that his face was marked up with doodles.

"Charlie, what is all over your face?" the boy's mother asked in a concerned tone as she helped him peel off his jacket and hang up his backpack.

"Hi, doggy," the boy gasped, keeping his attention on me. He wore a smile that stretched from cheek to cheek and exposed a large gap in between his two front teeth.

Layla dropped down to his eye level and inspected the doodles on his face. "Charlie, who wrote 'retard' on your face," she said in an instant burst of anger.

"Mommy, can I go play with the dog?" the boy questioned, completely ignoring his mother.

She ran out into the kitchen and grabbed a washcloth. After dabbing the rag under some warm water from the faucet, she returned with tearful eyes and began scrubbing the marks from her son's forehead.

Charlie didn't seem to mind. His bubbly little eyes were sparkling with excitement as he watched me sit in front of Layla and him.

When Layla was finished cleaning her son up of the marks on his face, she stood up and wiped a tear from under her eye, then smiled. "This is Linus, Baby, he is going to be staying with us for a while. Is that okay?"

"Yes," the boy said with glee. "Hi Linus, I am Charlie."

Turning to face his mother, he spat out a request so fast, I wasn't even sure it made much sense. "Mommy-can-Linus-and-I-go-play?"

Calming her face, which twitched back the verge of tears, Layla nodded and smiled. "Yes," she added with a laugh and a faint smile.

"Come on, Linus," the boy cheered as he took off into the living room.

I looked up to Layla, who was just looking at me with her smile, then I got up and followed the boy into the next room.

"Did you see where I left my Legos?" Charlie called out to his mother.

"Sweetie, they are where they have always been: right next to your bed."

"Right, Mommy but did you see where I left my Legos?" the boy repeated.

Dude, she answered you already.

She ignored his second request and focused on the typewriter before her.

The boy ran off to his room. The clicks of Layla's typewriter were slow and sporadic. After a moment of struggling to convey her thoughts onto paper, she tore a piece of paper from the machine and crumpled it up before she discarded it off to the floor.

I looked down at the ball of paper and gave it a sniff. I don't know why I sniffed it; out of habit I suppose. I gripped the ball and snuck out of the room so that I may find a spot to lay down and shred the paper into tiny little pieces.

I didn't get far, as Charlie stood in my way with a box of toys in his hands and a smile on his face. "Come and build with me, Linus," the boy suggested.

I found this, was just going to bring it to you.

I dropped the crumpled ball of paper and acted as though I were oblivious to its existence. The boy walked into the living room and I followed.

"I have been building a sailboat," Charlie said as he pulled a large toy out from the box. It was made up of hundreds of little blocks that varied in shape and size.

Wow, that actually does look like a boat.

I sat and watched the boy build with his blocks for hours on end. The look in his eyes of wonder and astonishment as he exerted his creative will evenly amongst each and every brick he lay was a marvelous feat to watch.

You know, Sam was a builder, too. I never really got so see him work, but I can only imagine he looked sort of like you when he did it.

"Charlie, come out here and eat dinner," Layla said from out in the dining room.

"Watch these," Charlie suggested as he climbed to his feet and walked out of the room. I followed.

"Is Memaw coming over tonight?" Charlie asked his mother as he took a seat in a chair that was far too big for him.

What the hell is a memaw?

"Yes. Mommy has to work tonight so Grandma will be coming over," Layla answered. While Charlie ate his peanut butter and jelly sandwich, Layla ran around the house frantically looking for something.

"What's wrong, Mommy?" the boy asked with a face covered in peanut butter.

"Nothing, Sweetie, Mommy just lost track of time."

A knock came on the door and Layla scurried over to answer it. She didn't bother to look and see who it was. She simply unlocked the door, laced up a pair of sleek black boots, and threw a jacket on over her clothes. An old woman walked inside. She wasn't smiling, and yet she radiated a sense of happiness.

"Hey Mom, Sorry, I didn't think that I was supposed to be to work until eight," Layla explained.

"Oh, it's fine," the old woman assured.

"Okay, well I really have to go," Layla said. She zoomed

over to Charlie and went to plant a kiss on the side of his face. She stopped when she noticed the mess of peanut butter he had made. "My God, Kid..." She pecked him on the forehead with her lips, then rushed out the door. "I am sorry," she reaffirmed to her mother.

"It's fine," the old woman assured her with a chuckle, then she closed the door behind Layla and took a seat at the table.

"Why hello, young man," the old woman said.

"Hi, Memaw," Charlie said with a mouthful of food.

"And who is this?" Charlie's grandmother questioned in noticing me.

"That's Linus! He is a dog."

"I see," the old woman said with a raised eyebrow and a smirk. "I didn't know you guys had gotten a dog. Mangy little mutt, isn't he?"

"Yeah," Charlie agreed with a laugh, though, in all actuality I do not think that he really knew what mangy meant.

A little mangy? I looked down to my coat and then noticed that she was, in all fairness, correct. It wasn't very long ago that I had taken pride in the cleanliness of myself. Somewhere I seemed to have lost track of that.

"Are you all finished?" Charlie's grandmother asked the boy.

"Yes," the boy confirmed.

What about me, I reminded them with beady, pleading eyes. I wasn't sure when I had eaten last. I wasn't really hungry, but not knowing when the last time I had eaten anything was, I felt as though I should eat something.

"Well, let's get you a bath and into PJ's, then you can play with your Legos before bed."

"Okay, Memaw."

The two of them went into the bathroom and Charlie took his bath. This left me alone in the house. I took the opportunity to explore a little bit. The small house was very empty. Aside from the regular bits of furniture, there wasn't much in the way of stuff to occupy the walls, corners, or shadows of the home.

I sat down in a cold, empty corner and let out a groan. It was clear that my life was no longer my own. Perhaps it never really ever was.

Chapter 12

All of the Things I am Grateful For

A few days passed by and a routine had begun to set in. Charlie would wake up and his grandmother would make him breakfast. Layla would come home at about that time smelling like too much perfume and sweat. She would alleviate her mother of her night's watch post and see Charlie off to school. This is where a big yellow bus would come into play. It would arrive in front of the house and take Charlie away. I was not sure why, but I never really liked that old bus. From here, Layla and I would go back inside. She would pass out until early in the afternoon, then wake up, make some coffee, and do work on her typewriter until Charlie arrived home from school.

It was strange to be on a downtime schedule in the mornings with Layla and then a sleep time schedule at night.

But being an adult, my reservoir of energy was depleted and I soon found myself not minding the extra tidbits of sleep when I could get them; especially given how much Charlie would tire me out with his love for playing.

The weekend had arrived, and that meant Charlie did not have to go to school. Layla sat on the patio of their small home that Saturday and wrote into a notebook with a pen that was far louder than most. Her presence was never quite that far, as she always seemed to have a need to be within eyesight of Charlie, even when he and I played in the yard.

"Okay, Captain Linus," Charlie said with a stick in one hand and a handful of leaves in another. He was wearing an eyepatch and trying to force his squeaky voice to sound deep. I simply watched him as he swung his stick at shadows. "Captain Linus, Aisha is hurt, get her back to New Horizon," the boy instructed.

Who is Aisha?

Charlie tossed his handful of leaves up into the air. The yellow and orange collection of blades rained down on us, but my eyesight remained locked onto his other hand. Just as I had anticipated, Charlie fired the stick he was holding as hard as he could across the yard. I sprung forward and landed on top of the twig just as it made contact with the ground.

Sam can throw much further, but for a boy who is one tenth the size of Sam, I guess that wasn't bad.

I brought the stick back to Charlie and he reached towards my mouth to retrieve it for himself, but I pulled back.

Woah, now.

"Come on, Linus. Give it back," the boy said with a giggle.

No, you just try and take it.

The boy laughed as I pulled the stick from left to right in an attempt to folly him. When, at last, he grabbed hold of the twig, he surprised me with his strength as he put up a fight. In the end, I was the stronger. He let up his grip in defeat and wrinkled his face in what I could only assume was a sarcastic expression of anger.

I trotted away victorious and pranced alongside Layla with my head held high and the stick in my mouth.

Hey, Layla, check it out. I got the stick.

Layla slid her glasses down to the tip of her nose so that she may look to me and laugh. She only wore the frames when she was writing or reading. She did not need them to normally see, which is something I thought to be strange.

That night, I slept on the floor in the living room near a spot I had grown comfortable with. While Charlie slept soundly in his room, I watched Layla sit on the couch and continue scribbling in her notebook. Whatever it was she was doing, she was struggling to do it well.

Suddenly my ears perked up and I shot up to my feet as both Layla and I heard the screams of Charlie coming from the other end of the little brick house. The level of intensity in the boy's screams were on par with the screams of the girlfriends that Sam used to see. It raised the hair on the back of my neck and I wasted little time. I bolted down the hallway and turned into his room where I found him sitting upright in his bed sweating and breathing heavily.

"What's wrong?" Layla said as she came in from behind me.

"Mommy, there was a man," Charlie let out as he broke into a full-blown cry. He was trying to explain how he had seen a man and that the man was harming his mother, but in between his sniffles and chokes of being overwhelmed with terror, Layla could barely understand him.

"It was just a bad dream, Sweetie, it's okay," Layla reassured.

The boy cried in his mother's arms for a few minutes while she cradled him and tried to ease his worry. I sat in the darkness of the room's entryway and watched. The glimmer of the moon's shine glistened into a small portion of the room, which lit up my face as my eyes locked into Layla's. It was in that moment that I understood that these night terrors Charlie endured were of a regular occurrence.

When Charlie had calmed down, Layla offered to stay with him, but he politely declined. After kissing him goodnight, she stood up and walked to the door.

"Can Linus sleep in my room tonight?" Charlie squeaked from under his covers.

Layla looked at me and then back to her son. "Yeah, sure, I guess."

"Come on, Linus," the boy called, sounding sleepy and frail due to the exhaustion of his mind.

I slowly walked over to the side of his bed, then glanced back to Layla to ensure all was well. She stood in silence, so I climbed up onto Charlie's bed and sat down. Layla left and Charlie began to pat my head as he looked to the ceiling with wide open eyes. After a moment of silence, he peeled his blankets off and sat up. The room was dark, but the moonlight granted us just enough visibility to see one another.

"You have a scar on your head," the boy said softly as the fingers of his little hands slowly drifted across the fur of my face.

I do.

"How did you get that scar, Linus?"

I got that one fighting a great and vicious demon. He was always more powerful than me, even to this day. But when the beast passed, I realized his death brought me no satisfaction and perhaps he never really was a demon at all.

"I have a scar, too," Charlie said as he lifted his shirt to show me his belly. Running straight across his stomach was a thick, discolored patch of skin. I pressed the tip of my nose against his tummy and he pulled away, giggling. "You've got a weird nose."

No, I don't.

"It's cold and all wet," he explained before laying back

down and burying himself in his blankets. It did not take him long to fall back to sleep while I sat by his side and kept guard. I was not tired and I knew that Charlie had chosen me over his mother to defend him that night because, unlike his mother, I could see the demons. They disguised themselves as shadows as they slowly moved about the room. I kept my eyes on them, but I did not fray. Not only did I know all of their tricks, but I also knew their strongest weapon was that of fear and doubt. I had neither, and in time, I too closed my eyes and slept beside my newfound friend.

***

The next few weeks were nice. I would keep Charlie company throughout the nights and see him off to the bus stop in the mornings, then I would sleep through the day with Layla until it was time to greet Charlie as he came home from school.

It was the morning of Charlie's last day of school before Thanksgiving break. Layla had taken some time off of work so that she may prepare her home and play the role of a hostess during the holiday that I knew little about.

"Charlie, get your jacket on, the bus will be here in a few minutes," Layla called from the living room, where she was dusting with so much attention to detail that it seemed a little crazy.

Charlie slid down from the seat he was in at the table. He had just finished breakfast and had a frown on his face.

My ears perked up to catch the sound of something shattering in the living room.

"Shit!" Layla moaned. She had dropped something- a vase, perhaps- and it had shattered in falling to the floor.

I ran over to the entrance of the living room where I picked up the scent of blood. Layla had cut herself on the glass and she was trying to stop the wound from bleeding, using her shirt.

"Are you okay, Mommy?" Charlie asked as he came up behind me.

"I am fine," Layla eased. "Mommy just needs a Band-Aid," she added while gritting her teeth.

From the looks of it, Layla had been trying to clean her house in such an obsessive way that she was doing more harm than good. She had started multiple tasks and projects, none of which had been completed.

As Layla rushed out of the room, Charlie turned to face me.

Are you ready, kid?

He put his jacket on, picked up his backpack and opened the front door. Layla was too preoccupied with addressing her wound to come and say goodbye, so Charlie allowed me to go outside first so that I may walk ahead and escort him to the end of the driveway; just as I had on all of the other school day mornings prior to this one.

"Linus?" Charlie asked. His head was hung low as he slowly shuffled towards the street.

Yeah, buddy?

"Linus, there is this girl at school named Fionna who is nice to me, and not many people are nice to me. I want to ask her to play with me, but when I tried a few days ago, another kid punched me in the nose."

What kid punched you in the nose? I will pee on his face if you show him to me. Does he ride your bus?

As the school bus approached, Charlie gave me a pat and then a hug.

See ya later, Kiddo.

"Bye, Linus," the boy said as he got on the bus and found a seat.

The school bus was filled to the brim with a couple dozen screaming little monsters. I watched one kid pull another's hair while a third spit on the window he was staring out of. I observed another child sit silently with his head against the glass and tears in his eyes. I noticed two girls kissing each other and thought it strange. I then spotted Charlie. He had found a seat near a window and had gone on to press his tiny hand up against the dirty glass. Amidst all of the chaos packed away inside of the yellow tin can, Charlie just sat there quietly and looked at me. He forced a smile as the school bus pulled off and disappeared out of view.

I sat at the end of the driveway for a few minutes and looked to the workings of the life outdoors. Things were mostly quiet. It was chilly and windy and there were more leaves on the ground than on the trees. While there was no snow on the ground, I did watch as minuscule flakes delicately drifted through the air.

I stood up and trotted back towards the house. It would take Layla a few minutes to realize I was waiting to come back inside, so I listened to the wind, which howled an eerie sort of moan. Whatever it was that troubled her must have been a heavy burden to bear. She was upset with something and, in turn, she sought to relay her sorrows to all those who would listen.

***

Two days later, Charlie was home from school for a vacation. It was Thanksgiving, and that meant that the day had arrived that Layla had been cleaning, cooking, and prepping for all week long.

Over the course of the next few hours, Layla's family began to arrive at the house. Her brother, Robert with his wife Monica and two kids, whose names I never learned, were the first members of the family to arrive. The two kids were teenagers: a boy and a girl who were much older than Charlie and thus had no desire to pay him any mind. Rob smelled of oil and grease, which left me to assume he did something with cars as a profession. His wife wore a sweet perfume in an attempt to mask her native scent of wine and sadness.

Next to arrive was Layla's mother and her husband. Layla's mother was at the house on most nights to watch Charlie while Layla went to work, but I had never met her husband before. He was an old guy with hairy ears. I didn't think that this was odd at first, because I myself have fur on my ears to keep me warm, but I soon realized that this was an abnormality in terms of what humans normally looked like.

As all of the guests sat around the dining room table, they chatted about their lives and inquired about the lives of others. It was clear that aside from Layla and the relationship that she had with her mother, not many of these individuals ever really saw one another.

A knock came at the door and Layla stood up to answer it.

"Here we go," Layla's mother added with a sigh. I didn't catch what their conversation was about prior to her sarcastic claim.

"Just be civil, Mom…. Please," Layla pleaded.

"I always am, Sweetheart. It's *him* that needs to not act a fool this weekend."

Layla opened the door and welcomed a burly looking man inside. He had big bushy eyebrows and an equally thick mustache. The man was accompanied by a woman who was skinny and attractive. While most of the house guests were well dressed in sweaters, button up shirts, and ties, this woman stuck out amongst the rest. She was wearing a low cut shirt that exposed her busty frame and she had a skirt on that I could almost see up.

"Laylee," the man said with glee. "You have met Clarissa, right?"

Layla, with a genuine smile on her face, gave the man a welcoming hug. She then raised her hand to wave at the woman. "Yes, we met last Christmas," Layla reminded as the authentic smile on her face dissolved into a fake one.

"Grandpa," Charlie squealed with glee as he ran up to the man.

"Hey-hey," the man said in his deep-toned voice as he hunched down to Charlie's level. "How is my favorite grandson?"

I caught one of Rob's teenage kids, the girl, roll her eyes.

"Good. Me and Linus built a spaceship this morning," Charlie said, grinning from ear to ear.

"Luis," Layla's mother's husband said as he stood to greet the man.

I knew that Layla's mother and father had been separated, but the addition of them now being remarried made the collection of characters in the home confusing to keep track of. I tried best to pay attention so that I may catch all of their names.

"Oh, hey there, Drew," Layla's father said sternly as the two men exchanged a firm handshake. The look in their eyes was that of two rival alpha males who had made a previous agreement of civility towards one another for the greater sake of the clan.

Drew sat back down next to his wife, Layla's mother, and then Layla's father, Luis, peeled off his coat and removed his shoes. Layla took the clothing off and away into a side room and Luis approached the table of family members.

Rob stood up to greet his father. "Dad," he said with a welcoming nod as he extended a hand for a shake. Seeing the two side by side, I noticed that both of the men looked a lot alike. Though Rob's father was a little bit thicker in his build, you could tell that Luis and Rob were related by blood. "Where are you guys staying?" Rob added as he stepped back to again take his seat at the table.

"Over at the Clarion."

"Ah, Nice," Rob said. "Place looks a little odd in between all of those old historic buildings eh?"

"Yeah, it kind of does," Layla's father said as he and his

thin wife took a seat at the table. "Windows are a little crooked, too," he added with a chuckle. "What about you guys?"

"The motel a few blocks down the street. It was the closest by. Monica gets a little anxious in the car after the accident."

Rob's wife, Monica, shot him a look that suggested she was annoyed at him for speaking of her in the manner that he had.

"Well, that's understandable," Charlie's grandfather eased. "How you holding up, dear?" he questioned, looking to his son's wife.

"Oh, I am okay," she defended. "I just get kind of nervous in long car rides, but it's really no big deal," she re-affirmed while tossing her husband a scowl.

Though my mind had synched up the scent of each family member with the visual picture of their face, it was difficult for me to keep track of everyone's name.

With everybody sitting at the table except Charlie, who was in the living room watching television, the members of Layla's family conversed on multiple subjects, the likes of which I had trouble following.

A few minutes passed and eventually the random pockets of discussion synched up into one greater conversation.

"Is he still carrying around that shredded rag of a blanket?" Layla's father asked while running his thumb and index finger through his mustache.

"Luis, stop it," Charlie's grandmother snarled in her old lady tone from across the table.

"No, it's okay," Layla eased. "He actually hasn't been. Since we got Linus, Charlie has been doing really well. There is no cure for his disorder, but having a friend in the house has really helped alleviate his symptoms."

"Well that's good," Layla's father said.

Layla stood up to go into the kitchen so that she may check on the food she had been cooking all throughout the day.

With her leave, the room dissolved into multiple discussions between the members of the family once more.

Rob's teenage daughter and Luis's girlfriend stood up from the table to go outdoors and smoke cigarettes. The rest of the group continued on with their chatter while I was left glancing from member to member trying to get a fix on the discussion.

This is stupid. Who does this?

Layla came back into the room and poked her head into the living room to check on Charlie before she sat back down.

"Say, did they ever capture that psycho killer, Laylee?" asked Charlie's grandfather as he began mouthing at a toothpick.

Why does he always call her Laylee? Her name is Layla. He of all people should know that; he is, after all, her father.

"I don't know, Dad. They said he fled out of town shortly after they caught on to him," Layla said as she exited the room to go check on dinner again. This time, her leave of absence did not result in a disbandment of the discussion. Luis had united the group into one single conversation with his question.

"Probably in New Mexico by now," Drew said with a frown.

"You hear about this guy, Rob?" Layla's father asked, turning to face his son.

"You kiddin'? From San Fran to Boston, it was plastered all over the news, day and night. The guy was carving up bodies in his basement."

"He was sewing pieces of them together to make a girlfriend," Rob's teenage son said, entering the conversation. It was the first thing I had heard the kid say since he had arrived earlier in the day.

If his monotone voice were any more flat, I'm not so sure that he would even have a voice at all.

"That's some sick shit," Rob said as he poured his wife another glass of wine.

"Language, Robert Meeker O'Strander," snapped Layla's typically passive mother from across the table. Her new husband bulged his eyes and jumped back as if poking fun at her outburst. This made Layla's father chuckle as he continued fiddling with the toothpick in his mouth.

Wish I had one of those when I was teething as a pup. Sam never let me chew on things.

"Turkey is done," Layla announced to the house of guests. "I will go grab anyone on the patio. The rest of you grab a seat."

Rob's daughter and Luis's wife were still outside smoking cigarettes together. It seemed strange that a teenage girl appeared to relate so well to an old man's wife.

The family gathered around the table. Smiles and laughter filled the room. Layla had pulled it off. Her family was together under one roof. All of these people, strange and sour at times, were united for the sake of family and friendship.

The smell of the turkey that Layla had been slow roasting since early in the wee hours of the morning watered my mouth with aspirations of devouring the magnificent bird. I walked into the kitchen to scope the status and there it was! The first time I had actually managed to lay eyes on it all day. It was moist and still steaming. The skin was a perfect golden brown. Herbs and spices were sprinkled on the uppermost side to bring the masterpiece even further towards perfection.

Layla walked out into the dining room with plates of food. I heard her ask her father if he wished to help her cut up the bird so that it may be served.

I sprung up against the counter to check the turkey out first hand and get a better smell of the thing. My God, was it gorgeous. Like angels descending from heaven with cups of wine and platters of cheese, the slow cooked bird was simply a marvelous creation, a true gift from God.

I heard Layla walk into the room and squeal. I could not look up to face her. I dropped the chewed up, mangled corpse of the turkey from my mouth and backed away slowly.

Layla stumbled backwards. She was in complete and utter shock for a moment. She was fighting back the urge to release a stream of tears as best she could, then the levees broke and the undammed water uncontrollably poured down her face.

What was I thinking? I let my primitive instincts get the best of me for thirty seconds and in that time I managed to ruin Thanksgiving for this entire family.

Layla's father walked into the room and chuckled "The Bumpus Hounds." I did not get the reference. "Well how was it?" he continued with a laugh.

His comedy was not welcome and I felt no better in the slightest for what I had done. I snuck my way towards the door. Unknowing yet of what I had done, Charlie saw me.

"Do you wanna go outside, Linus?"

Yes, oh God, yes I do!

He opened the door and I slid out, taking off for the woods.

I will run away. Yeah, that's it. I will go back to the farm and find Tess's son and break him out of that prison.

I didn't get far. In fact, I only made it to the tree line. I was close enough to still see the house, yet far away enough to not have anyone see me.

I sat down in a pile of leaves and licked my paws till they were sopping wet, then cleaned the flavor of turkey off of my face with them. Despite feeling ashamed for what I had done, I still felt a sort of lust for the flavor of the bird.

I'm a monster, I thought with a sigh.

The two homes that towered over Layla's had chimneys that were bellowing smoke up into the sky. They were warm homes with happy families.

Those families mustn't have a dog, and if they do, certainly not a dog that ruins everything.

Layla's home didn't have a chimney. It had a dog. Me. A selfish monster of a beast that deserved nothing. The ruiner of nice things and a destroyer of happiness.

I should leave.

Chapter 13

Lights, Camera, Action!

I spent the night in the woods and woke up to see a few of the family's women, Layla and her mother, niece, and sister-in-law, all pile into a black SUV.

Where are they going at this hour? The sun isn't even up yet.

I made my way out of the woods and across the yard to the end of the driveway so that I could watch them drive off. All of the lights in the house were still off.

That's odd.

Something rifling about in the bushes across the street captured my attention and I set out to investigate. As soon as the shrub stopped shaking, I stopped moving. After a second or two it rattled again, so I continued with my inquiry.

Hissing and screaming like a maniac, a cat pounced out

from the bush and swiped me across the face. It had completely caught me off guard. I whined and jumped back.

Ow, what the hell?

I could smell the blood on my face. The little shit had cut me good. Luckily, I had been quick enough to flinch and close both of my eyes, or else I would have found myself losing one in the attack. I made way for a tree line off to the side of the house that faced ours. I took a seat among the brush to lick my paws and attempt to soothe the pain in the laceration on my face while watching the sun rise.

"Linus," a young voice called from across the street.

My ears twitched in hearing my name and I crawled forward on my belly to investigate. Charlie was in the front yard of his house. He couldn't see me hiding in the shrubs across the street, but he was out looking for me.

"Linus," he called out again, cupping his fingers around his mouth to increase the level of sound his voice made.

It's best you just go and forget about me now, Charlie. I only serve to disappoint everyone I meet. Everyone ends up miserable or dead.

A small blue car pulled up to the neighbor's house. A tall, thin woman dressed in a brightly colored blouse got out of the car and walked up the sidewalk to meet a man who was loading electronics into a van.

"Linus," Charlie yelled once more. His voice cracked midway through the call as his emotions got the best of him for a second.

"Little boy. What are you doing?" the woman asked as she stopped to notice him outside yelling like a rooster early in the morning.

"I have lost my dog," Charlie said with a very concerned look on his face.

"I see." She turned to face her male friend and said, "Jimmy, get the camera out of the van."

"We really have to get uptown, Cass. We are already

running late as is," the man argued.

"This will only take a minute," she softly eased before turning back to face Charlie.

The man came over with a large camera and a microphone. He handed the woman the microphone then took a few steps back and harnessed the camera up onto his shoulders. He then looked through the viewfinder and stood firmly in place like a statue.

Wow, movie makers. Charlie is going to be a celebrity.

"Little boy, what are you doing?" the woman asked, now holding her microphone in between Charlie and herself.

"You already asked me that," Charlie pointed out with a raised brow.

"Just cut that part out," she informed her cameraman with a laugh. "We will start from scratch here in a second.

"I'm going to interview you and put you up on TV. When people see the video, they may wish to help you find your lost dog. Would that be okay?" she asked.

"Sure," Charlie answered.

"What's your name, little boy?"

"Charlie O'Strander," he said sternly.

"And what are you doing out here, Charlie O'Strander?"

"I'm looking for my dog. He ran away last night after eating the turkey."

"He ran away after eating the turkey?" she confirmed with a laugh.

"Yeah. My mom cried, but my uncle Rob said that things like that make a holiday more memorabilia."

"Memorable," she said, correcting him with another light chuckle. "And he is right. Sometimes crazy things like that do make a holiday more memorable." She turned to speak directly into the camera. "Sometimes throughout the chaotic orchestration of gathering a family together for the holidays, things go wrong. When they do, we just have to take a deep breath and relax. The holidays are stressful enough as is, and when all's said and done, the events we interpret to be catastrophic end up being laughable nine out of ten times when we look back on them." She turned back to face Charlie. "So tell us, Charlie. What is your dog's name?"

"Linus," Charlie said.

"And what does Linus look like?" she pressed.

"He has black fur with a brown neck and belly. He also has floppy ears, a scar across his face, and a wet nose that can tickle you when you touch it," Charlie explained.

The reporter put her free hand on Charlie's shoulder then looked directly into the camera again.

"While everyone is out shopping on this Black Friday, fighting over deals on products that they don't really need, while the middle east is being nuked into the stone age and Americans face the highest suicide rate the country has ever seen, Charlie O'Strander is out looking for his dog. It's something as simple as the bond between a boy and his puppy that can remind us all of the true joys to be found in the fragile life we all share on this planet.

"He is not a puppy. He is a grown up dog," Charlie pointed out.

"Oh yes, but of course," she affirmed looking down at Charlie and then back to the cameraman with a smile. "Let's go ahead and cut it there, Jimmy."

The man holding the large camera lowered the heavy-looking piece of equipment and placed it into the van alongside many other gadgets. He pulled a laptop out of the vehicle, then hunched down to his knees so that he could better focus as he typed away on the computer.

"Charlie?" Layla's father called as he came outside to discover the boy was speaking to a stranger. As he drew near, he must have sensed that the woman possessed very little threat as he lowered his tense posture and eased his stiff look. "Who are you?"

"Cassandra Clark," the woman introduced with an

outstretched hand. "Mister...?" Her pause insinuated this was a game of fill in the blank.

It took a second for Layla's father to catch on. He shook his head and answered, "Oh... O'Strander! Luis O'Strander," he said as he extended one of his muscular arms and shook the lady's hand.

"Well, Mr. O'Strander, we want to run a little piece on Charlie here searching for his dog if that is alright with you."

"On the television?"

"You got it, will only end up being a two or three-minute piece, but I think it's cute, and people should find some joy in watching it."

"Um, well, yeah, I guess so. As long as it's alright with you, Champ," Charlie's grandfather asked, looking down to the boy who simply gave a nod and a faint smile in affirmation.

"Excellent. Maybe this will help with finding your dog," the reporter added with a smile. "Jimmy here is going to have a few consent forms for you to sign off on quickly and we should have this up and running with the ten o'clock broadcast."

The man, Jimmy, who was messing with the laptop near the van stood up and approached with a clipboard. "John Hancock right here and here sir."

"That it?" Charlie's grandfather asked after obliging with the signatures.

"That's it," the reporter confirmed with a smile.

"Cass, we really have to get uptown or else we will be in a deep world of shit," the cameraman said with a sense of urgency after looking at the watch on his wrist. He glanced up to see the woman beaming an angry gaze into his face.

"*Language*," she spat.

"Oh right, sorry," he said looking down to Charlie and then up to his grandfather.

"Oh, it's okay, this kid has heard way worse," Charlie's grandfather said with a chuckle. "Come on, kiddo, let's get you inside. Your uncle Rob is making breakfast and I don't want him to burn your mother's house down.

"But we have to find Linus," the boy begged.

"We will. Let's just get some food in us so we can get out there and look, okay?"

"okay," Charlie hesitantly agreed.

"Goodbye, Charlie," the reporter said with a smile as she turned to hop into the van and take off with the man that accompanied her.

Without saying anything, Charlie simply waved goodbye to her as he too turned away to walk inside with his grandfather.

I crawled out from the safety of my vantage point across the street.

I am sorry, Charlie.

Just as the boy's grandfather placed a hand on the doorknob, Charlie turned around. His eyes slowly scanned over the yard.

Did he hear me?

Unsure as to whether or not the boy would see me, I sat frozen upright in place. Charlie lowered his head as he accepted defeat in losing me. Just as his facial expression fell into sadness, it also lifted into joy and excitement.

"Linus!" Charlie squeaked out in glee as he noticed me across the street looking at him. Never before in my life have I ever seen someone more excited than Charlie was in that moment. He ran as quickly as his little legs would carry him towards the road.

The sound of a car coming down the street caught my attention and I was quick to piece together what was about to happen.

No, Charlie stay!

"Charlie!" the boy's grandfather screamed in horror as he ran after the kid.

In that moment, no single physical object or phrase would stop Charlie from running towards what it was his fixation was locked onto. In his mind, he had to reach me and there simply was no other option.

As the car continued down the street, I sprung up and ran towards the road.

If I can make it across before him, I can prevent his brains from being splattered all over the asphalt street.

I had little time to think. Everything was happening so quickly, and despite me running faster and harder than I ever once had before in my life, I felt like my feet were being weighed down by cinder blocks. Demons were near and they wanted me to fail in saving the kid. As the car came closer, it looked as though the demons may be granted their wish. I had made it to my end of the street at the same time Charlie made his first step onto his end of the road.

No, please, no!

I shifted all of my weight into taking the longest strides I could manage, and then pushed myself further.

Please, no!

The beams of the car's headlights lit up both Charlie and I as the car's driver slammed on the brakes. The brakes squealed to life as they tried to halt the car, but the speed in which the vehicle traveled was too fast. It would never stop in time and I put everything I had into one final leap.

I soared through the air towards Charlie who, despite facing his imminent demise, still had a smile on his face. My front paws made contact with Charlie's chest. I bent my knees and lowered my head to shift my momentum. As I fell into the boy, I pressed up on him with all of my strength so that I may lift him up and off the ground. The car was just seconds away from smashing into the two of us and it looked as though the demons who grasped at my feet were going to win. I closed my eyes and continued pressing up against the boy with all of my strength as both him and I flew through the air. I felt a gentle push against my backside and the speed in which me and Charlie drifted through space was accelerated by a minuscule fraction. Someone, or something, had given me the extra amount of momentum I needed. Maybe it was God, or perhaps it was the angels who work through the goddess I knew as the wind. Either way, a higher power was in our presence and had fought off the evil that conspired against me.

Charlie and I landed in his driveway and rolled to a stop. Both of us gathered a collection of scrapes and cuts as we slid against the ground. The driver of the car that almost hit us sped up and drove off without ever actually stopping.

"Oh my God!" Charlie's grandfather yelled as he reached the two of us. "Are you okay?" Luis yelled as he dropped down to the ground.

Charlie was laughing and petting me. He seemed oblivious to the fact that the two of us should, in fact, be dead roadkill.

We went back inside and spent our morning in the living room. After facing what looked to be a certain death, I was okay with relaxing with Charlie and his family.

A few hours later, Charlie's grandfather gathered everyone around the television. Just as he turned the channel to his desired location, Layla and the other girls in the family came home.

"Laylee, get in here quick!" Luis yelled.

Layla entered the room with a smile on her face. She was holding bags of stuff that she had purchased on her morning adventure out with the other women.

Everyone was watching the television and as Layla joined in, the smile on her face quickly dissipated away as it shifted to a frown.

"Why," she said calmly as her eyes bulged from their sockets in her head and the look of terror overtook her face. "Why is my son on the television?"

"Yeah, neat right?" her brother, Rob, said with a chuckle.

"No," she said as a tear gently rolled its way down the front of her face. "It's not neat," she added with a sniffle. Then her tone shifted to that of anger as her eyebrows squished together, "Why, is *my son* on the television?"

"Woah, relax, Laylee. He was looking for Linus and the lady thought it would be nice to do a little piece on it," Layla's father reassured.

"And who the *fuck* gave her permission to do that?"

"Okay, Charlie, come help your memaw make your bed," Layla's mother said as she set down the packages that she was holding so that she may escort Charlie by the hand to his bedroom.

The boy turned back and tossed me one of his gentle smiles. "Come on, Linus," he said with a squeak.

I followed with my head hung low and my tail tucked between my legs. Charlie was oblivious to the anger that filled the room and was just happy to have me home. But anger was an emotion that had an overwhelming impression on my senses.

"I did," Layla's father said with unyielding confidence.

As Charlie entered his room with his grandmother, I stopped at the corner of the hallway to turn and watch over the family in the living room.

Another tear followed the path of the last as it made way down Layla's face.

"And who are you, Dad, to think you can make that call?"

"What's the big deal, Layla? It was sweet," asserted Luis's wife. She was trying to calm the situation.

"*You,*" Layla denounced as her eyes bolted over to pierce through her father's young wife. "You can stay *the fuck* out of this!"

"Hey, come on, now!" Luis objected. He too was losing his temper, but in that moment, Layla's frustration could be matched by no man.

"It's no secret that you did a shit job of raising us, *Dad.* You don't get a second *fucking* chance with *my fucking* son!"

The room went awkwardly silent after the statement was made. Most everyone, not directly involved in the conversation, drifted their eyes to the floor to show that they had no desire of being a part of the discussion.

"Just get out of my house," Layla said as a third tear made its way down the side of her face.

"Layla, I-" Her father tried to defend himself but was quickly cut off.

"Take your *fucking* whore and get the *fuck* out of my house!" Layla screamed. Her voice crackled like lightning as it ripped through the air and caused me to flinch.

I think it's time for me to join Memaw and Charlie in the bedroom.

I quickly jogged the rest of the way down the hallway and placed a paw against Charlie's closed bedroom door. His grandmother cracked the door open and peaked out. When she saw it was me she ushered me inside, then closed the door again. Charlie was sitting on his bed playing with some action figures.

"Are you hungry, sweetie?" his grandmother asked.

Yes! I wagged my tail with a smile, excited to eat something. *I am famished.*

"Yeah," Charlie passively answered. He continued playing with his toys as if afraid to break focus.

"OK. Stay in here and play with Linus for a little bit and I will go make you something to eat."

"Okay, Memaw," Charlie answered.

As she left the room I heard the front door of the house slam and some glass shatter followed by a high pitched, hair-raising scream. It was not one of physical pain or torture like I so often had heard living with Sam, but rather a screech of frustration and anger. At some point in the conflict, Layla had snapped and simply lost it.

I turned to look at Charlie and realized that he too had heard the scream. His eyes were watery but, harnessing courage that I did not know he had, the little boy suppressed his emotions and smiled as he ran his fingers through my fur.

"Let's build a fortress to hide inside of," Charlie suggested as he began stripping the blankets and pillows from his bed.

Yeah, that sounds like a great idea.

Chapter 14

Dead Leaves and the Dirty Ground

After a weekend of Charlie and me stowing away from the drama that was Layla's family, life returned to normal. The coming weeks were mostly pleasant. It was a low-key lifestyle lived with my two best friends. A truly deserving duo of attention, love, and affection, Charlie and Layla were a light that I had found amidst a very dark and lonely night.

Whilst napping in the living room, I awoke to the smell of tart cherries. Layla had baked a pie and, while I despised fruit, it certainly smelled delicious. The tingling sensation in my bladder suggested to me that I needed to go outside. This also reminded me that it was about that time for Charlie to come home as well. I had trained myself to go outside and go pee both when he left for school, and when he returned.

"Going to go wait for Charlie?"

Every day.

She opened the door and I flew out into the crisp autumn air. It smelled as though late day snow showers were inbound. I quickly took a leak in the grass against a small prickly-looking bush, then took a seat upright in the driveway as I glanced down the street for Charlie's bus.

I noticed a white truck sat running idle across the street. A man was inside. His eyes scanned over our home. After a minute or two, his attention was captured by the yellow bus that approached from down the street.

The bus came to a stop and Charlie got off. He had a smile on his face as he noticed me waiting for him. It was funny how happy he would get to see me each and every day. It was as if every interaction we had was still also the very first. His love towards me never seemed to diminish.

The bus pulled away and the man inside the truck squinted his eyes and furrowed his eyebrows as if he were confused. Charlie was hugging me and had his back to the man in the truck. While I was sitting upright with my eyes locked onto the alien that lingered outside our domain, Charlie was oblivious to the stranger who gawked.

The door behind me opened. It was Layla.

"Hey, Baby," she said, greeting Charlie, who was still clenched tightly around my neck.

He let loose of me and greeted his mother with a wave. He then returned to patting me on my head. I ignored the sweet gesture as I maintained my stare at the man who sat in his truck. The man then got out and leaned against his vehicle as he continued watching over us three. He was wearing a checkered button-up shirt and jeans. He looked as though he hadn't showered in a few days. A messy, unkempt beard disguised most of his face. His hair was long and greasy-looking, and it hung down into his eyes.

The sky darkened as clouds set in for their watered assault over the land. The man progressed up the driveway and, after a moment, Layla seemed to recognize our strange visitor. Shoelessly, she jumped down onto the asphalt driveway and placed a hand on Charlie's shoulder.

"Baby, get inside," she said calmly with terror in her voice.

"OK. Come on, Linus," he said, tugging at my collar.

No, I think I better stay.

"Charlie, get inside and call nine-one-one! *Now!*" she flared with a fear induced rage.

This was the very first time I had ever heard her yell at her son like that. It was just cause though, given the anger, the hatred, and the overall presence of evil I felt swirling to life outside as the man drew near.

The hand that ticks away the seconds of a clock came to a stop. The gears in my brain had aligned and shifted into place. I could see clearly who this man was. It was someone I myself hadn't seen in quite some time. It was Sam.

Sam? ... You're alive! What the hell? I don't even recognize you. Where have you been? What are you-

Before I could finish my thought, Sam lifted his leg and stomped down onto my snout. My face gave off a loud cracking sound that reverberated through my entire body. I yelped and squealed as I tried to squirm my way out from underneath his boot. What a fool I was to stand directly in the path of his attack. Sam twisted his leg and smeared my face further into the asphalt. Again, I cried.

With a strength that I did not know she possessed, Layla picked up a large pot of sickly flowers. Long since neglected and dying, the pedals of the dried out plant fell to the ground as she heaved the pot filled with dirt at Sam.

"Get the fuck away from us!" Layla screamed.

Sam blocked the blow of the flower pot with his forearms. The pot shattered, covering both him and I in a heavy collection of black dirt. Though her attack did nothing to deter Sam, it did serve to redirect his focus. Sam lifted his foot from my face, moved towards Layla, and left me to whimper in pain on the ground.

"It has been quite some time, hasn't it," he said coldly with a grin. "I did not even know that you were still living around here. And a new dog? How did you come about finding him? What are the odds that you would?" he added with a chuckle.

"Get away from us. I swear to *God* I will fucking kill you!" Layla screamed as she lunged for a piece of the broken pot.

Sam leaped forward and stepped on her hand with the heel of his boot just as she grasped a piece of the glass. He slowly began rolling his foot. Her fingers broke with the sound of many cracks and she was forced to drop the shard of glass as she yelped out in pain.

Now towering over her, Sam harbored a smug smile. "I just cannot believe you live around here. I thought you were long gone, but when I saw your boy... Charlie, was it? When I saw Charlie on the television and heard his last name, I put all of the pieces together." He dropped down to her level and placed a hand firmly on her shoulder as he looked directly into her eyes.

Layla clenched her fist and swung for Sam's face, but he seemed to know that it was going to happen. Using his free hand, he caught her fist with his and twisted her arm around until it cracked. She screamed as her level of torment accelerated.

"I am sure that you have heard the terrible things they have said about me on the television. I just want you to know that I never truly cared for those girls. I thought that you were gone and I was trying to recreate you using the very best of them. I only chose the features of them that closely resembled yours!"

He took her by the wrist of her broken arm and raised her up off the ground. She kicked her legs, but he pulled her in tightly to counter her tantrum of terror.

"Sounds silly, looking back on it all. They never came

close to your beauty." He paused to kiss her bloody hand. She cringed as he smeared the blood from her fingers across his bearded face. "But at last, here you are. You and I are together again," he added with closed eyes...

With a look of hopelessness, Layla began to cry.

"That look. That look right there," he said with a taunting sense of emotion. "I have sifted through a half a dozen women in search of that very look," he added with delight.

Then, out of nowhere, he snapped back the fingers of her good hand and pitched his forehead forward, smashing it into her face. The sound of Layla's fingers cracking and breaking was accompanied by her horrific screams as Sam simply laughed with pleasure. In head-butting her, he had also accomplished opening up a cut just above her eye, which was quick to run blood down the side of her face.

My eyes, nose, and mouth were in a monumental amount of pain from being kicked directly in the face. Never in my life have I felt the physical level of agony that I perceived in that very moment, but I knew what this moment was. I knew who Sam was. I knew who Layla and Charlie were. And I knew who I was.

Coming to my feet, I exposed my teeth and began to growl. The hand that counts the seconds on the clock within my brain had continued its ticking. Louder, I growled as blood and spit dripped from my face. I sounded like a complete and total maniac. A feral wolf lusting for the scent of blood, my insanity forced Sam to stop and drop Layla as he turned to face me. Just as his eyes met mine, I, for the first time, saw something within him I had never once previously seen; the look of fear.

I lunged through the air and the fist of Sam's right hand caught the side of my face. The blow tossed my head off to my right, but it did not stop the momentum of my weight as I landed on top of him. Together, he and I fell to the ground. He struggled, swinging and kicking at me. While his attacks landed in their destructive right, I was unharmed. In that moment, my strength was unmatched, as I harnessed the power of a thousand years of ancestral bloodlust. Ignoring his struggle, I tore through the flesh of Sam's face and pressed forth with my assault. In a last ditch effort to deter me, Sam reached into his pocket and withdrew a knife. He flipped the blade open with his thumb and then stuck the weapon deep into my side. He then pulled the blade out so that he may stick me again, but Layla pitched forward and grabbed his wrist. He cut into her mangled hands with the blade and she screamed as it took every bit of strength that she had to try and restrain his arm from stabbing me again. Despite my severe wound, my pool of energy was limitless as each snap I made with my mouth ripped a deeper incision into Sam's face. I tore away strips of skin and meat from his cheeks, then moved on to the area around his neck. I continued until he stopped moving. His face was mostly undefinable, ground-up meat. His eyes were still intact. Covered in blood, they were as wide as could be as he slowly choked out on his own blood and struggled to breathe. I had torn open his neck. With my lips still raised and the blood of my enemy dripping from my teeth, I looked directly into Sam's eyes and watched closely as the last few seconds of his life ticked away.

With a grotesque amount of flesh, meat, and blood covering my face. I seized my feral look of insanity and just tried to regain control over my breathing.

Layla and I looked at each other over the dead corpse of Sam. In that moment, I had no words. She must have thought a monster of me, but then she did something that surprised me. She reached her broken and bloody hands around my also bloody mane. She pulled me in tight and buried her face into my fur, which served to muffle her cries and cover her in more blood. I rested my mouth on the back of her head and just sat there with her as she cried.

Two cop cars came screeching up the street. The lights on both vehicles were flashing brightly. No sooner after the first car stopped did a cop jump out the driver's side door and sprint up the driveway towards us. He had his pistol out and trained on the scene of blood and gore. A second, older looking cop approached from behind him with his pistol holstered. He looked down at Sam's mangled corpse. With wide eyes, he turned to the other officer and leaned in to whisper something that I could not hear.

After hearing the man's secret, the younger officer holstered his weapon and went back to his car to begin chatting into his radio.

"Ma'am, are you hurt?" asked the older officer as he crouched down to us.

Layla loosened her grip from around my neck so that she could turn to face the cop. Her hands were twisted and broken badly. A few of her fingers even exposed bone and ligament tissue as they continued to seep blood into my, already, wet coat of fur.

"Ma'am, do you know this man?" the officer asked as he helped Layla up to her feet.

With a blink, she gave a simple nod.

"How do you know this man?" he pressed.

"He is the father of my son," she said with tearful eyes.

"You two were together? How long ago was that?"

An ambulance and two more cop cars screamed their way up the street.

"About ten years ago. We were never actually together. He raped me when I was a senior in college." A fuse set off an explosion of emotions as her tears ran wild. Though her mouth hung open, no sound accompanied her cry. The officer put a hand on her shoulder, and she fell into his arms.

It was my job to protect both her and Charlie, but knowing she needed the warm embrace of human interaction, I simply sat by the side of the two while the officer comforted her. The cop's eyes drifted over to meet my bloody face and, in that moment, both he and I thought one and the same.

Good dog.

***

I received many stitches to address my wounds. My battle scars troubled me with aches and pains, but paled in comparison to the torment brought on by a permanent limp that I now had. I tried best to disguise my pain. I did not want either Layla or Charlie to know of my greater injuries. Though I was immune to the pains of Sam's kicking, swinging, and stabbing at the time of his demise, my body was broken and sore in the coming days after the conflict. After some time, I got used to the of pains in my bones and accepted them as a regularity to my state of being. It was a small price to pay in the wider spectrum of things.

That coming winter, Layla was different. She was quiet and secluded with her emotions as she reflected on the intricate thoughts that troubled her mind. It was a puzzle that only she could decipher and deal with. She played more of a role in keeping Charlie always near to her and even joined in playing with him almost as much as I had. I played my role in keeping both of them company and excelled in lifting their spirits when Layla would be forced to attend to her own mental needs.

Both Charlie and I spent the days, from sun up to sun down, playing. Every day was something different with him. Be it flying spaghetti monsters, firemen, or characters from his favorite comic book, Future Winds, the boy simply loved to play. Though I grew tired earlier and earlier each and every day from trying to keep up pace, I did my best to never show signs of fatigue when he wanted to play.

I remember very little from that Christmas. For some reason, my memory seemed to be slipping out from under me from time to time. I recalled a lot of family coming over to the house that year. A lot of hugs were exchanged between all members of Layla's tribe; even those that didn't particularly like one another. I remember Charlie having experienced a wonderful holiday. Family members showered him with lots of love, but I was tired. Too tired to partake in much of anything. At one point, Layla's father had offered me a chunk of turkey from underneath his side of the table, but I just can't seem to remember if I had taken him up on the luscious offer or not.

Winter was gone and Spring had once again arrived. While the snow and the cold were disappearing away to unveil a much more pleasant, comfortable day, my bones ached.

Every breath I took felt heavy on my lungs. While I felt as though I could not get enough air, I did not panic and gasp for more. I knew that losing my sense of cool would do no good in serving any benefit to me.

Layla was sitting at the table in the dining room tapping away at her typewriter. Every stroke was a spark of life on paper. She must have fallen into a creative rhythm, as she typed faster than I have ever heard her go at it before.

"Hi, Mom," Charlie said as he entered the room, dressed and ready for the day with a head of wet, messy hair.

"Good morning, Sweetie," Layla welcomed as she continued to focus on her work.

Charlie squirmed his way up into a chair and sat at the table beside his mother. He picked up the top page from a stack of papers to Layla's right side and read the words out loud.

"Emotive, a story of life, love, compassion, and chaos."

The words caught Layla's attention. "No-no," she worryingly warned. She stopped typing and placed a hand on the stack of papers to stop the boy from digging any deeper into the story that she was crafting.

"Can I read your book, Mommy?" Charlie asked with a big smile on his face.

"Maybe when you are older, Sweetheart," she answered with a faint smile of her own.

"But Mommy, I am getting very good at reading."

"I know you are, Sweetheart, but this story, it is not for you to trouble yourself with. At least not now," she comforted with a kiss on his wet forehead.

"Oh, hey, Linus!" Charlie said as he turned to notice me and escape from the chair where he was being barraged by the kisses of his mother.

I began to lick his face and he fell back on his bottom laughing. How did he not see that coming?

You can run from your mother, but you cannot run from me, Charlie.

"I just took a shower, Boy," the child laughed.

Well you missed a spot, had to get that one for you.

Layla continued with her work and I followed Charlie out into the living room where he began stuffing blank pieces of paper into his backpack as if they were grand important documents needed for a meeting.

My legs began to buckle out from underneath me. I was in so much pain but, in a ploy to disguise my torment, I took a seat and watched the boy as he continued in his readiness for the school day to come.

"Can I tell you a secret?" the boy said, leaning in with a whispering tone.

Sure, Charlie, whatchya got?

"Today, after school, I am going to play in the stream down the street with Fionna," he whispered.

My memory tripped out from underneath me and I was unsure if I had heard what he had said, or if he had even said anything at all.

Charlie hugged me and gave me a kiss on the tip of my nose, which was comforting. He then walked away.

Suddenly I felt as though I was freezing and yet, somehow, as if I was standing in the center of a volcano. I am not sure how someone could feel both extremely hot and extremely cold at the same time but, in that moment, I felt exactly as such.

"Okay, Mom, I am off to school," the boy cried out as he put on his Spiderman sneakers and pulled the straps of his matching backpack over his shoulders.

Layla stopped typing and walked over to the door to plant a kiss onto the side of the boy's cheek. "Have a good day, Sweetie."

"Mom," he groaned. "I don't like those."

"Yes, I know," she admitted, "but I just love you so dearly."

My legs shook in pain as I tried to get up to walk the boy to the bus as I always did, but then I found myself aimlessly standing in the yard.

What was I doing here? How did I get here? Where is Charlie? Did he already leave?

The early spring weather was cool and crisp; new life budded on the trees that lead down the street in a planned path of beauty. A full year of work was in store for life, to bear flowers and fruit would be a task against the odds, as it always was. A task that was driven by eons of instincts for the will to survive. They would prevail as they always did, I was sure of that, but I was tired; exhausted from a day that had only just begun.

Unsure of my own motives, I walked up into the woods behind the house. The forest from this point on stretched for miles and, well into the day, I walked aimlessly until I found what it was that I was searching for. It was a spot between two large oak trees, whose leaves of last season were sprawled out across the ground like welcoming blankets on a chilly morning. Light shone through the clouds and helped to warm this particular spot.

A soothing comfort washed over me, it pleaded for me to lay down and enjoy the sun's rays for just a bit. I resisted the urge at first, but ultimately gave in. I gandered up to the sky to see clouds pass overhead that took the form of familiar shapes and silhouettes. I could see Kyle and Mary. They embraced each other tightly, as if intending to never let go of one another ever again. I was filled with a soothing sort of warmth as I watched my two dear friends love one another in the sky. A few minutes passed and then the clouds churned to paint another picture. It was Tess. She and her child frolicked through fields of tall flowers alongside a team of horses. Their pace was majestic and steady across the glowing afternoon sky. Tess stopped in her run to look at me and smile with her big beady eyes. She then went off to chase after her calf. The clouds shifted into a third and final image. It was the face of Charlie, smiling and laughing as his mother held him tightly within her arms. He reached down to me with his hand but vanished before he could touch me.

I closed my eyes.

A redwing blackbird summoned himself up into one of the great tall oaks above me and I slowly glanced up to him with my eyes while keeping my head flat on the ground. He gracefully sung me a comforting song; one that felt familiar to me, though perhaps I had not actually ever heard the song before. It reminded me of the visions I used to have as a very young pup. Visions of my siblings. Visions of my mother and the place where she had raised me for a short while before Sam had come to take me away. In the distance I could hear more birds chime in with songs of love and affection as I painlessly closed my eyes, just one last time.

Made in the USA
San Bernardino, CA
25 September 2018